WICKED CHILL

A WICKEDLY SPICY FAIRYTALE RETELLING

WICKED EVERMORE
BOOK THREE

INES JOHNSON

THOSE JOHNSON GIRLS

FORBIDDEN FOREST
THORNHALL
GREYM
SNOW KINGDOMS
FENVALEN
VALEBR
RAVENHOLD
COASTAL KINGDOMS
TIDEHAVEN
IN
SEA KINGDOMS
EVERMORE

CURSED REALMS
BEAST LANDS
DOMS
REST
FIRE ISLANDS

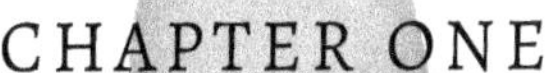

CHAPTER ONE

The storybooks would make one think that all girls want the same thing: the fairy tale. A charming prince to love them, to provide for them. Rescue them. That might be how the story starts after the happy ending. But the fairy tales never tell little girls what goes on in the middle of the stories.

In the beginning, the storybooks promise magic. A glass slipper. A spinning wheel. A single dance that changes your fate. They whisper of once upon a times and happily ever afters as if love is a crown and marriage the throne. The prince arrives at just the right moment, says all the right things, and somehow—without even knowing her name—he loves her.

But in the middle?

In the middle, the heroine gets pricked by a thorn.

Fed a poisoned apple. Put to sleep while the prince goes off on his… let's call them adventures. Then the story skips to the end. The spell is broken. True love's kiss is given. Happily ever after commences. And the page goes blank.

In the middle, princes stray. At the center of it all, men lie. They spend late nights out at taverns or at war. When they're at home, they leave their dirty stockings on the bedroom floor before they climb in, rut on their tired wives, and then turn over on their backs to snore without checking to see if she achieved her pleasure. Most times she did not.

Damsels, princesses, and little girls were sold raw deals by fairy tales. If they learned the truth, it would not be to swoon over the prince but instead to make a play for his castle.

In a castle, the walls don't wander. The hearth never lies. The roof shelters. The layers of brick endure. The structure will stand firm in the face of battle, never asking its inhabitants to shrink. In the storybooks, the castle is never the villain. It is always the safe haven for the fairy princess. It offers its spine of stone and marrow of secrets. A castle will keep a girl warm when the king grows cold.

Queen Raveena of Everfrost stood in the highest turret of Thornhall Castle. The wind coiled around the turret like a serpent, hissing through frost-rimed stones, whispering rumors through the arrow slits. Raveena stood against the biting cold, her cloak a shroud of midnight blue that snapped at her ankles. Below her, the courtyards burned in golden torchlight, alive with murmurs of wedding proposals, of soldiers returning from war, of joy, of surrender.

Her fingers curled around the ledge's worn stone, the ice beneath her touch slick and biting. She welcomed the sting. Far below, on the polished flagstones of the western walk, her stepdaughter smiled up at a charming young prince.

Snow White stood in a pearl gown embroidered with the silver thread of innocence. A sash of deep sapphire cinched her waist, the same solemn blue as a morning sky. Her sleeves, sheer and pale as snowdrifts, shimmered with frosted lace, while a single red ribbon crowned her hair—a pop of blood in a kingdom of white. She looked every inch the naïve maiden from a storybook illustration, all softness and virtue, as though she hadn't spent the last three years quietly sharpening her smile into a blade.

She laughed softly, delicately, one hand at her throat, the other resting lightly on her suitor's forearm —as though she hadn't spent the last year after her father's death weaving a net from pity and perfection.

Prince Charming stood beside her in all his golden glory—chiseled jaw, broad shoulders, trim waist wrapped in royal blue velvet that matched hers. His smile gleamed with practiced brilliance. His lips were the kind that made a girl wish for a curse just so she could bite them. He looked like he'd stepped out of a stained-glass window, every inch the hero of a tale that rarely told the truth.

Raveena's gaze narrowed, fixed not on the prince but on the girl clinging to his arm like she was the prize. She was playing the role perfectly; the grieving daughter, the dutiful bride-to-be, the unsuspecting heiress.

Raveena saw through it. Snow had been born to steal. She wasn't after the prince. She was after the one thing Raveena loved most.

Not the man.

The castle.

Raveena tilted her head, watching them from her perch like a hawk considering prey. A prince and a princess. A storybook illustration. The stuff girls were told to long for, to train for.

Be lovely. Be docile. Be desired. Be chosen.

Chosen.

What a brittle, breakable thing.

Snow turned her face away, laughing into her shoulder just like Raveena had done with Snow's father years ago. She'd thought she'd caught the girl spying during her seduction.

With Snow laughing, that was when Prince Charming looked up. His gaze swept the turret as if summoned, pausing until it landed squarely on Raveena's shadowed perch. He was too far to make out the color of his eyes, but Raveena felt the weight of them all the same—bright, amused, and burning with that awful male confidence that made women believe their every word in a grim fairy tale.

He tilted his chin, subtle, practiced. A man who had offered that same look to chambermaids and noble-women alike. A smile curled at the corner of his mouth, slow and secret. It said: *I remember how you tasted. I remember how you begged.*

Raveena hadn't begged.

Well—she had. Because nothing swelled a man's pride more than a husky plea. But she hadn't meant it.

Men like Charming needed the illusion first. A little breathy desperation. A few well-placed sighs. They needed to feel in control, to believe they'd conquered something that had already laid itself bare.

It was the same game it always was. She'd played it before—played it well enough to win herself a crown, a castle, a kingdom. Charming thought he was the most powerful player on the current game board. The fool boy was playing checkers where every move was a straight line and every piece played the same role until it reached the other side.

This was chess—a game of queens. Queen Raveena was the powerful piece on the board. Moving diagonally, vertically, horizontally—any direction, so long as it served the game.

The king, for all his glory, was slow. Limited. One square at a time. If he fell, the game was over.

The king might end the game, but the queen decided how it was played. She moved in all directions, saw all angles, set the traps and triggered the end. Take her off the board, and the rest would crumble—slowly but surely. Not because the game was over. But because the fight had already been lost.

Raveena's first husband's death and her empty womb had revealed that pitfall. In the matriarchal Snow Kingdoms, it was the daughters who inherited. Raveena was a widow, not a mother. So her crown, the kingdom, her safe haven, would pass to the last remaining daughter.

Raveena had tried to shape the girl into a queen. In those early days, when she still believed her belly would swell with a true-born princess to solidify her claim to Everfrost and Thornhall, she had been… patient. She had offered Snow lessons in statecraft, in subtext, in how to wield a smile like a dagger and read a room with her eyes half-lowered.

The young princess had shrugged off those lessons with the ease of someone who believed she'd never need them. She'd birdwatched through strategy meetings. Replaced poisons and politics with ponies and pouting. She hadn't wanted to play the game. Eventually, Raveena had stopped trying to teach her.

Right now, her stepdaughter was making a classic mistake. She'd taken her eyes off the prize. Princess Snow had her back to her intended. She reached up to a love bird in a tree to offer it a seed. While she did, the man who was supposed to be courting her licked his lips as he gazed up at Raveena.

Raveena should have turned. She should have stepped back into the dark. She should have reminded herself that she was a queen and not some half-starved mistress hoping to be seen.

But she didn't.

She let him look.

Let him want her.

The wind caught her cloak and snapped it behind her like a banner, hair blowing loose from its pins in white, silken strands. She didn't cover herself. Didn't soften her stance. She stood there, high above them all, frozen and radiant and cruel.

Let him see what he'd touched and abandoned. Let him remember what it felt like to be devoured by her lips. Let him think, even now, that she might still allow him back into her bed, into her body. Let him remember that she would do things that a little girl would never do, never even imagine a man would want.

If Raveena could tempt him, seduce him, possess him, marry him, she wouldn't have to step down from her throne. The ceremony would change. The bride would change. A single name scratched from parchment, a crown passed not to the daughter but to the stepmother.

Raveena would do anything to keep this castle. Even get on her knees for him again. And when she dropped to her knees and got her hands on him, he would be the one begging her.

She would do it. She would do anything to keep this castle.

Its hearths. Its vaults. Its black stone halls that remembered her footsteps and echoed only for her. Its banners bearing her crest. Its magic woven through the very foundation like marrow in bone.

To keep the castle, she needed the prince.

To keep the prince, she needed to win him.

Prince Charming, for all his gilded grins and practiced touches, was no king. He was barely even a pawn. But pawns could still be useful.

They cluttered the board, got in the way, distracted, defended. They moved only forward, in simple, direct lines. Which made them predictable. Which made them easy to sacrifice.

Still, Raveena needed him to think he was the one leading the charge. That was the true art of the game. Making a man believe he was in command while maneuvering him exactly where you wanted him. A queen did not seize power with brute force. She took it with elegance. With patience. With blood, when needed.

Snow turned back then, placing her hand gently on the prince's chest. His smile shifted, dimmed as though a fire had been doused by, well, snow. He didn't look at Raveena like that: warmly. He looked at her like he was on fire and liked the burn.

That was fine. Lust would win out. It was with lust that he looked at her. Not Snow.

Snow looked up and caught sight of her stepmother then. The girl offered her a shy smile, the same smile she'd offered when Snow had come into her home shortly after her mother's death. The same smile she'd offered as her father said his vows to her new step-mother. The same smile she'd offered after they'd laid her father to rest in the ice.

Raveena returned the same smile to her stepdaugh-ter. One that was slow, deliberate, polished to perfec-tion. It was a queen's smile. All poise, no warmth. Not a greeting, not affection. The kind of smile one might give a rival across a ballroom—or a pawn across a chessboard.

The smile lingered just a moment longer before vanishing like breath against glass. Queen Raveena turned on her heel and headed back into the castle, her fingers trailing on the stone like the caress of a lover.

If she could not win the prince's heart, then she'd have to take the girl's. Take it by force. Better a kingdom stained in red than a crown lost to a simper.

CHAPTER TWO

Graham ducked his head as he stepped into the warmth of the tavern. The door creaked behind him. It swung shut on a gust of wind that carried with it the sharp mineral tang of melting snow and the coppery scent of cold steel. Inside, it was loud. Tankards slammed against tabletops. Boots scraped against old wood. Fire crackled in the hearth.

He paused, letting the warmth hit his shoulders, letting the noise roll over him.

He was back. Home. But his bones didn't know it yet. Neither did his instincts.

He scanned the room like a man still expecting a troll's axe in the dark. The war had done that. Not just the blood or the marching or the beasts that screamed in the night—but the meetings. The war councils. The endless circle of crowned heads and princeling strategists with hands too clean and voices too high-pitched from dicks whose balls had yet to drop.

They'd drawn their maps and moved their markers like boys playing kings. And Graham? He'd been the pawn.

He and his men—the best warriors Everfrost and Fenvalen had to offer—were tossed into choke points and ravines, asked to hold ground while nobles argued over who would take credit.

Most of the time, Graham had nodded along in those councils, quiet as a shadow. Then he went out and did what needed to be done.

The monsters they faced in the dark forests didn't care for politics. Trolls didn't answer to thrones. But Graham knew how to kill them. So he'd made his own plans, issued his own orders, and let the kings believe their brilliance had turned the tide.

Let them keep their illusions. Graham didn't care what princes thought. Not in Everfrost. In his realm, the male nobility were decoration. It was the queens who moved the real pieces.

Inside the tavern, he'd barely taken two steps before someone spotted him. The cheer hit him like a fist.

"Graham Huntsman! The returning conqueror!"

A roar followed, chairs skidding, men rising,

laughter booming. Suddenly, he was in the center of it. Hands clapped him on the back hard enough to bruise. Ale was being shoved into his grip. Women pressed in too close with breath that smelled of cider and false promises.

He smiled because it was expected. Nodded because it was easier than speaking. Let them sing of his deeds in the Troll Wars—their verses uneven, their stories half-wrong but told with the conviction of men who hadn't seen what he had.

They made him a legend in their cups. He let them. It was easier than telling the truth. That he'd been a coward. That he'd run.

Not from the trolls. No, those grimy beasts he'd slayed with far too much enthusiasm. He'd run from here, from his home. And before daybreak, he'd be running again.

The laughter grated. The fire was too hot. The press of bodies made his skin itch. He hadn't been touched in years, hadn't wanted to be. Now hands kept brushing his arms, his shoulders. A woman's palm dragged across his thigh as she leaned in, lips close to his ear.

"You look strong enough to split mountains, Huntsman," she purred.

He gave her a ghost of a grin, raising his tankard. "Mountains don't scream."

She laughed, not getting it.

Graham shifted on his stool until her hand was off his thigh and he'd given her his back. He gave all of the tavern his back and hugged his ale close to his chest. He took a long swallow of drink. It was bitter, earthy, almost sour. It did nothing to quiet the hum beneath his skin.

Every time the tavern door opened, his muscles tensed. His eyes snapped to the entrance. A boy delivering firewood. A messenger from the garrison. An old woman looking for her son.

Not her.

Of course not her.

He turned back to the hearth and pounded the bar for another draft. Then another.

Getting drunk wouldn't solve his problems. Nothing would, except to hightail it out of here at first light. Though at the rate he was drinking, he would tip over ass first within the hour.

Too bad. She loved his ass. Or had loved his ass. She probably hadn't thought of it in the last three years.

The door opened again. This time, a young couple walked in, arm in arm. They looked at each other the way poets wrote about in songs. Her cheeks were pink from the cold, his hand protective on the small of her back. They laughed at something only the two of them could hear. The warmth of their joy cut through the winter gloom of the tavern like sunlight through frost.

Graham curled his lip at the sight. He'd thought himself in love once. What a farce.

Fairy tales didn't happen to men like him. They were written for the silk-skinned sons of noble houses and boys born to crowns they didn't earn. Princes won princesses. Princes had even claimed a common girl or two and lifted them from ash to ballgowns, gave them slippers and songs and kingdoms.

There were no fairy tales for men with blood under their fingernails and scars where medals should've been. No castles for the wolves who fought the battles, only cages or exile. No bedtime stories ever ended with the soldier getting the queen.

Graham turned back to his ale, the mug heavy in his hand, the bitter taste settling on his tongue like truth. She wouldn't lower herself to walk through that door. Not the girl who had once kissed him in the shadows behind the castle stables, hands in his hair like she couldn't breathe without him, only to marry another man.

For power. For a crown. For a bloody castle.

Another cheer broke out as a lieutenant staggered in, carrying a silver trumpet. "To the castle! The parade's almost begun!"

Soldiers rose, half-sloshed and puffed with pride, adjusting their sashes and wiping mead from their beards. One by one they made for the door, boisterous and ready to bask in the adoration of a grateful kingdom. A grateful queen.

"You coming, Huntsman?"

Graham didn't look up. Just shook his head.

"Why the hell not? You're the reason we survived that fool war. All these men owe you their lives. The queen—"

"Go on." Graham cut the man off before he could say her name. "Celebrate. You deserve it. An old, tired man like me just needs rest for his weary bones."

They scoffed at that. Graham was in his prime, but he felt ancient. Aside from not wanting to see her on her throne, out of his reach, he didn't want to rub elbows with any more of the pale, porcelain sons of the north, all silk-lined collars and flaxen hair that never seemed to tangle. He was broad where they were narrow, sun-dark where they were snow-pale. His hair was black as coal and always too long, curling damp at the nape of his neck. His voice was rough, and so were his hands—callused from blades and blood and breaking through ice that never melted fast enough.

He didn't have the kind of muscles sculpted for show, the kind court women liked to admire from a careful distance. His were built for work. For hauling, hunting, dragging half-dead men from the battlefield. Built for pinning a woman down and making her forget her breeding.

The matriarchs of the Snow Kingdom liked their men delicate. Pretty things they could sharpen their wit against or crush beneath their polished boots. But every so often, they wandered into dark corners to have a bit of the rough.

Just enough dirt to remind them what power tasted like when it begged.

Just enough to ruin themselves—quietly.

She had come to him like that at first. But she'd kept coming back. And like a fool, he'd let himself believe she wasn't just using him for the bite. That maybe—just maybe—she'd meant it.

He shot out of his seat. The stool clattered to the ground and cracked, the wood splintering. He couldn't stay here. If he did, he knew he'd get ensnared back into her trap. He wouldn't be gone by morning. He was leaving now.

Graham laid a few tarnished coins on the ale-stained table—more than enough to pay for the drink he hadn't finished, the stool he'd broken, and the praise he didn't deserve.

He downed the rest of his ale in one long swallow. It burned on the way down, bitter and sharp, like regret aged in oak. He didn't flinch. He turned to go.

"Huntsman?" Behind him, a voice cut through the din. Thin. Reedy. Too nasal to be born anywhere but behind velvet curtains and cushioned chairs.

Graham didn't answer. Just turned and glared.

The man's throat worked, and he shrank into himself a bit. He had to clear his throat once, twice before resuming. "Her Highness begs an audience."

CHAPTER THREE

The late king's room was a shrine to masculine austerity—dark woods, heavy fabrics, and a chill that not even the roaring hearth could quite chase away. The bed dominated the space, a towering monstrosity of carved ironwood with a headboard etched in the crest of Thornhall: a roaring stag framed by thorns. Its posts rose like blackened branches, twisted and regal, holding up the sagging canopy of blood-red velvet. The bedding was thick, serviceable, a palette of storm-gray and oxblood—no frills, no softness, no invitation. It smelled faintly of old smoke, waxed leather, and the ghost of a man who had never quite lived up to the throne he'd claimed.

Raveena stood before the looking glass on the wall in her late husband's chambers. Tall and unforgiving, the mirror's silvered face stretched nearly floor to ceiling, framed in black iron thorns that curled like barbed wire. It reflected her with brutal honesty—no magic, no illusion. Just the cold truth of her face, her figure, her crown. Each night it had been in her line of sight as her husband had mounted her and performed his duty. She'd taken those five, sometimes ten, minutes to regard her reflection and look for flaws in the dark.

Morning light spilled pale and merciless across the marble floor. The snow-filtered sun showed everything: the shadows beneath her eyes, the faint bruise along her jaw, the bloom of a blemish rising like a betrayal just beneath her left cheekbone. Things had gotten a little out of hand in last night's bed sport.

She lifted a gloved hand, fingers bare at the tips, and summoned a current of cold magic through her veins. The mirror shivered. Frost bloomed in delicate veins along the edges of the glass. Her reflection stared back: cloud-white, high-boned, pale eyes like a storm over deep water.

The blemish marred the illusion. Not large, but noticeable. Her face had always been nearly symmetrical. *Nearly* was the danger. Any flaw became obvious by comparison.

Raveena exhaled slowly, pressing her fingertips to the imperfection. The skin beneath her touch tingled, tightening and smoothing as if the magic were ironing out time itself. The swelling receded. The color cooled. A perfect canvas once more.

She stepped back, checked the angle of her crown, and adjusted the tilt of her head. Her gown was slate-blue velvet, trimmed in silver fur, cinched just enough at the waist to hint at softness while promising steel beneath. The bodice framed her shoulders like armor. The sleeves shimmered with ice-thread embroidery—sigils of her line, symbols of frost, thorns, and flame.

Stitched just above the curve of her left wrist, subtle but deliberate, was the silver silhouette of a wolf mid-prowl. It was not the proud, antlered stag of Thornhall but the emblem of Fenvalen—the frostbitten kingdom of her birth, where wolves ruled the woods and queens ruled the land. A reminder of where she came from, of the blood that still ran wild in her veins.

When the Queen of Thornhall passed into the veil, the old king found himself with a daughter too young to claim the matriarchal throne and an army too feeble to defend it. He needed a bride—strong, cunning, and from a bloodline with teeth. Raveena had been one of many princesses paraded before him, but she was the one who stood her ground, who spoke of alliances not as favors but as contracts. While others fluttered lashes, she laid out strategies. While they simpered, she hunted.

She didn't win the king's heart. She won his hand.

And with it, a kingdom. Now she might lose it all because of a barren womb.

If Raveena had borne a daughter to her late husband, she would have married her stepdaughter off to some faraway kingdom, and the throne would've passed peacefully to Raveena's daughter. But her womb had betrayed her. And now her back was to the wall.

The key was Charming.

She looked from the mirror to the bed where he'd lain with her just last night. He had moaned her name like it meant something. Gripped her hips like she was the only woman he'd ever touched. She'd made the boy howl his pleasure—and gods, he'd howled.

A simpering miss like Snow White couldn't do that. Couldn't even imagine that her cuny could perform such acrobatics on a male's cock. Snow had all the appeal of a pressed flower—white and soft and quietly wilting. Untouched, untried, untested. The kind of girl a man tucked on a shelf and praised for her virtue while sneaking off to find a woman who knew what to do with her mouth. A woman who knew how to make a man forget his own name.

Raveena had made him forget. Unfortunately, Charming remembered his duty the next morning. The boy had stumbled back into his obligations, murmuring some apology that sounded too much like his mother's voice to be his own thoughts. Back to the little heir in her dove-gray gowns and breathy politeness.

Raveena could stomach a great deal. But not being discarded. Charming may have scrambled out of bed last night, but that glance this morning told her that he wanted more. She knew how to keep him wanting. Knew how to manipulate his pride, his hunger, his need to prove himself a man beyond his mother's leash.

Charming didn't want Snow. He wanted approval. A throne. A crown. He just didn't know yet that the fastest path to all of that was still through her.

He was a boy playing at politics. She was a queen who had survived them. If he wouldn't choose her outright, she would simply go over his big head instead of putting his little head in her mouth. That, after all, was the art of ruling men—reminding them they had power only so long as it served their queen.

Raveena turned from the mirror and walked through the halls of the palace with her head high and her cloak trailing like storm clouds behind her. Her guards opened the double doors to the parliamentary chamber. The hush that followed was immediate.

The Parliament of Snow convened but once a year. A gathering of crowns to discuss borders, alliances, and wars, both current and future. Treaties would be signed, broken, and rewritten before the ink dried. Promises would be made in one breath and gutted in the next. Behind the formalities, behind the icy pleasantries and diplomatic airs, another kind of hunt would begin: the marriage mart.

Princes, young and old, would be paraded like prize stags. Their mothers showed them off, counting muscle and scars like coin. Some were eager, some reluctant. All of them dangerous in one way or another.

And among them: Charming.

With his golden army, his honeyed tongue, and that smile he gave like a favor. If he married Snow— godmothers help them all. Snow, who held birthright to this castle. Snow, whose bloodline would give her claim and whose new husband and his regimented soldiers would give her the means to seize it. Snow who was weak and would let this castle fall easily into the hands of a cunning queen mother with obvious ambitions.

Dozens of women turned to look at Raveena as she strode to her place at the table. Not one woman smiled. They were exquisite, every one of them. Eyes lined in charcoal and cunning. Some wore crowns of white gold. Others simple circlets. Some wore no coronet at all yet carried more power than empires.

There were no men in the room. Here, the queens ruled. Here, the knives were at the ends of perfectly manicured fingertips.

Raveena's gaze swept across the chamber, calculating and cold. She wasn't looking for smiles. No one here wore them sincerely. She was searching for the most symmetrical face in the room—the one that had haunted paintings and parades, lullabies and lies.

She turned to a passing attendant, a mousy thing in livery too stiff for her narrow shoulders. "Where's Snow White?"

The girl startled at the question, nearly dropping the tray of crystal goblets she carried. "I—I believe she was last seen in the stables, Your Majesty. Tending to the animals."

"Of course she is," Raveena said dryly. Of all the places to be when power was gathering like a storm—Snow had chosen the hay.

"Queen Raveena, how lovely of you to finally join us. We were beginning to worry. At your age, one never knows when a simple cold might take a turn for the... inconvenient."

Lady Charming sat beneath a tapestry of her house's crest, gold thread glinting in the firelight. The sigil—a falcon mid-swoop, talons poised—loomed behind her like a quiet threat. Her gown was plum silk edged with ermine, her jewels ancestral and ostentatious. She wore no crown, but her bearing made one unnecessary.

"And you, Lady Charming, are as stately as ever. One might forget you've stepped back from courtly affairs."

"Stepped back?" Lady Charming sipped her mulled

wine. "No, no. A wise woman simply learns to rule from the shade."

"A wise woman also knows when to step into the light. Especially when the stakes rise higher than her… reach." Raveena finally spared the woman a head-on glance, looking down her nose at the smaller, plumper woman with a few wrinkles around her eyes that magic could no longer hide.

"Yes, well. The strength of a kingdom is rarely decided in a throne room. More often, it begins in a cradle."

Raveena's smile didn't falter. "Cradles break. Thrones endure."

"Not without an heir. Not without a legacy. Forgive me—your reign has been most... singular."

"My stepdaughter still has some rearing needed before she finds a castle of her own. Meanwhile, when I wed again, the daughter I bear will inherit this castle."

"You plan to take another prince? At your advanced age?"

"One of the reasons I sought you out, as you had your magnificent son when you were ten years my senior. A fine prince your son is. But I imagine he still needs a firm hand to guide him. Not a young thing like my stepdaughter."

"Young things are soft. Malleable. I think my son would do well with something fresh."

"Then he should marry the queen who already holds the scepter."

The two women regarded one another with the politest of glares. Their smiles were small. The threats behind them loomed large. Hands folded in practiced poise, yet their fingernails gleamed—sharp and ready to strike. The air between them was quiet, but their teeth were bared beneath civility, ready to bite.

A sudden burst of horns split the air. The sound was sharp, bright, ceremonial. The brassy call echoed through the stone halls, followed by the distant roll of drums. The fanfare of heroes.

"Your Majesties, Highnesses, Graces and Ladies— the soldiers have returned from the Troll War. The procession is entering the city gates. The parade is set to begin."

A rustle moved through the gathered court, a flutter of interest and the gleam of opportunism. Outside, the courtyard erupted with noise: cheers, the clatter of hooves, the clash of steel and celebration.

Lady Charming turned, all composed grace and calculated delight. She touched her throat as if in reverence. "It would be ungracious not to greet our heroes. I must pay my respects."

Lady Charming glided away, her gown whispering behind her like a well-kept secret. The horns sounded again—closer now, fuller. The other women followed the sound, moving toward the fanfare.

Raveena didn't move. She waited. Once the chamber was empty, she turned and slipped away down the hall opposite the procession.

She didn't need to see who had returned. She wasn't ready to know.

If he stepped off one of those horses, still battle-worn and broad-shouldered…

If he didn't swagger into the castle gates, scarred and sun-darkened, wearing the memory of her like a wound…

No. She wouldn't go out there. Wouldn't stand among the queens, pretending not to care. Wouldn't search the sea of soldiers for his face and pretend not to ache when she saw it.

Or worse—when she didn't.

Instead, she turned swiftly, silken skirts whispering against marble, and disappeared down a side corridor, her shadow vanishing like a secret between the stones.

CHAPTER FOUR

Graham pressed his back to the cold stone wall, breath held tightly in his chest as two palace guards rounded the corner. Their boots clicked too sharply against the flagstones, voices echoing like they'd forgotten this place was once a fortress, not a parade ground.

He barely needed to hide. That irritated him more than it should've. Thornhall Castle's defenses were still garbage.

All the good men—the real soldiers—had volunteered for the Troll Wars. The ones who stayed behind were the peacocks, the polished and perfumed, the kind who worried more about the fit of their uniform than the weight of their blade. They had ceremonial swords and ceremonial spines to match. They guarded paintings and paraded through gardens. Ask them to defend the crown from a real threat and they'd fumble the draw.

The guards paused just a breath away from his hiding spot, idling beneath the shadow of a frost-rimed arch.

"You been out to the stables?" one asked, sniffing the air.

"Nah. Why?"

The first wrinkled his nose. "Something smells like horse."

A curl of straw clung to the front of Graham's coat. He plucked it loose with rough fingers and flicked it away. Damn. He should've cleaned up before going to her. But he wasn't planning for this to be a social visit.

The guards moved on, still talking, oblivious to the wolf in their midst.

Graham exhaled. Slow. Controlled. Then he moved.

He stuck to the walls, weaving through the inner corridors with muscle memory older than war. The servants' passages hadn't changed. Neither had the little cracks in the castle's security. The noble lords might have layered new gold over the banisters, but they hadn't patched the foundation. The castle might gleam on the outside, but it still creaked beneath its own weight.

Graham had been in enough strongholds to know that most castles were built the same. Same spine of stone beneath the keep. Same drafty great halls echoing with power plays. Same winding passages meant for servants and spies alike.

The turrets always offered too many blind spots. The ramparts too few guards. The cellars always held more than wine. Secrets clung to the mortar like moss, hidden in plain sight for those who knew where to look.

Once you knew how to slip into one, you could slip into them all. At least Fenvalen had been manned by wolves—men with sharp teeth and sharper instincts. Thornhall, by contrast, was guarded by deer. Pretty creatures with polished antlers and glossy coats, more concerned with ceremony than defense. They pranced instead of prowled, preened instead of protected.

He passed a column carved with old frost runes and ducked behind a tapestry, emerging into the side wing near the royal chambers. The air here smelled of snow lilies, the scent she always wore, no matter the season. It hit him in the chest.

If he hadn't known the way by memory, he would've known it by following her scent. He didn't have to think. His body remembered every step, every turn, every breathless moment along the narrow hall to her door.

He'd only walked this path once before. Just once. That night had etched itself into the bones of him. Burned itself into the backs of his eyes. It still visited him in dreams. It was his only recurring nightmare.

The last night. The worst night. The night before her wedding.

She'd called him to her chambers in the dark, cloaked and silent. No words. Just mouths and hands and desperation. He'd made her beg. He'd made her cry. He'd never been sure if they were real tears or just the result of the intense pleasure he'd delivered her. She'd kissed him like a confession, left him naked and aching in her bed, then married another man at dawn.

Graham had left so he wouldn't commit treason. Whether it would've been to wring the elderly king's neck or hers, he would never know.

The same corridor now stretched before him, silent and gilded, mocking in its memory. He took one step. Then another. And then—there it was. Her door.

He stared at the golden knob for a long moment. Then his eyes shifted to the left. The adjoining door just beside it, the one reserved for the king. The one the old bastard would've slipped through at night to perform his royal duties.

How many times had the old man touched her before going toes-up? He'd had three years. Had he taken her every night? Or maybe he'd only come to her just before her monthly courses when she would be most fertile.

When they'd been together, Graham had still come to her on those nights. But they'd done… other things aside from him entering her body and joining themselves in the way he'd believed they were destined to remain. It hadn't mattered to him that she wouldn't let him put a baby inside her. He'd selfishly wanted to be the only one inside of her.

Fool.

Graham had been halfway through the southern front when word reached the battlefield: King White was dead. Poison, illness, a fall—no one seemed certain. What Graham remembered most wasn't the shock. It was the shame.

His first thought hadn't been for the kingdom. It had been for her. That she needed him. That he should be the one holding her.

Pathetic. And yet—here he was. Back again. Covered in hay and horse stink and regret, standing in front of her door like no time had passed at all.

He opened the door and entered like he belonged there. There was no one to stop him. Even if those deer old guards tried, they'd fail. Because Graham was on a mission.

He wasn't sure what he'd expected. Velvet and furs, maybe. Royal pomp. Gold-framed portraits of herself, or the late king, arranged just so in memoriam. But this…

This wasn't the room of a queen.

It was hers.

All Raveena.

Neat, to be sure. Everything in its place. But not life-less. The fire had been lit recently; the scent of snow lilies and heated stone lingered in the air. Curtains half-drawn let in strips of pale light that stretched long and cold across the floor.

Strategic stations dotted the room like a general's war chamber. Puzzles. Riddles. Layered games of strat-egy. Tables crowded with playing pieces mid-turn, some frozen in triumph, others stalled in the thick of battle.

He drifted toward the chessboard like a man approaching something sacred. She'd set up a masterful game. White side—her side—led with a solitary queen. No bishop, no rook to hide behind. Just a few pawns and the queen, moving sharp and clean across the board, poised to strike.

Black side had more pieces. Power gathered. The king was advancing.

At first glance, white would win. She always did. He remembered that. She'd talk while she played—distract him, seduce him, keep her hand on his thigh while she lured his pieces into ruin.

But then he saw it. One move. Just one. If black's knight moved to E5—sliced right through the board—it would be over.

Graham's mouth twitched. It was almost the exact board from a game they'd played back in Fenvalen. She'd been so certain she had him then. He'd made that knight move with a lazy grin and taken the win from her with a single flick of his wrist.

Could it be the same game?

Could she still be obsessing over that loss?

There was a whisper of a door opening behind him—the one that connected her chambers to the king's room. He didn't reach for a weapon. Didn't need to. He knew it was her.

The air shifted. That scent—frost, lilies, a trace of something wild—drifted in.

She stepped through the door—and froze.

Even paler than usual, if that were possible. Her eyes locked on to his like she was afraid to blink and miss him. She didn't scream. She didn't call for guards. She just stood there, drinking him in.

And gods, he let her.

Her gaze touched every part of him: hair damp from snow, boots muddied from stables, shirt tight across his chest. Her eyes lingered longer than they should've. Always had.

Her cold glare burned hotter than a fire. The corner

of his mouth curved, slow and sardonic. Then, finally, she spoke.

"Graham."

Raveena took a single step forward. That was when Graham pulled the dagger and aimed for her heart.

CHAPTER FIVE

Raveena moved forward with the slow, deliberate grace of someone who had long since learned that fear was the first scent predators picked up on. His blade didn't stop her. She walked right up to it, let it touch the place where her heart was rumored to lie, where her pulse beat just beneath skin. The steel kissed her flesh, parted it with a whisper, and left the smallest, singing sting.

She didn't flinch. Didn't blink. Didn't even breathe.

She only felt the warmth. And maybe a pinprick of pain. It had been so long since she'd felt anything at all. Not since he'd left her.

"You're alive," she said, her voice quiet and crystalline in the hush of the chamber. She didn't say his name again. It tasted too close to prayer.

"I could kill you," he growled.

Raveena's eyes fluttered shut. Gods, how she'd missed the sound of his deep timbre. No one had a growl like her Graham.

There were nights over these last three years where she'd walked into the woods alone, trailing the scent of her own magic just to lure something wild close. She'd listened to the wolves howling beneath the frost-heavy trees. She'd close her eyes, pretending. The wolves would howl in warning, but none dared approach her. They were too smart to face a predator far higher up the food chain.

None of them sounded like him. None of them made her body shiver with need while feeling soothed at the same time. None of them made her ache.

Raveena opened her eyes and reached for Graham.

He flinched at her touch. The dagger pressed against her throat. The skin broke cleanly this time. A bead of blood slipped down and disappeared into the hollow between her collarbones.

"You have no protection," he said, voice low and furious. "Anyone could walk in here and take your life."

Still ignoring the blade, Raveena touched his face. Her fingers brushed the edge of his cheek, where stubble scratched against her palm—coarser than she remembered. He'd always kept his beard neater in their youth, trimmed close like a soldier reporting for duty. Now it sprawled in wild defiance, like the man himself.

She lingered there, letting her touch trace the rough line of his jaw, then the curve of his cheekbone. There—a faint scar she didn't recognize. Another near the temple, pale and puckered, half-hidden by a curl of dark hair. Her thumb grazed beneath his eye, where shadows pooled like bruises. He hadn't been sleeping. Not well.

Neither had she, though she hid it. Her magic kept the signs at bay—smoothed the sleepless nights, blurred the grief of loss. But the ache still hummed in her bones.

Her fingers twitched with the urge to heal him. To smooth the scar tissue, to erase the sleepless hollows, to press magic into his skin until it glowed like it used to. But she didn't. He hated that—being made soft by her touch, reshaped by her will.

"I like the beard."

"Raveena!" he barked.

Her lips curved into a sulk. "Don't yell at me."

Graham pulled the dagger back by a breath, his grip tightening. "I nearly slit your throat, and you're upset because I raised my voice?"

He looked at her like she was an unsolvable riddle. Like he'd never wanted to touch something more and never been more afraid to do it.

Raveena turned her back on him with imperial calm. She walked toward the vanity like she hadn't just stood on the edge of a blade. Because the bite of the steel had barely registered as she reveled in the return of her lover.

A single drop of blood slid down her neck, stark against pale skin. She studied it in the mirror, eyes tracing the delicate red curve with almost academic interest. Then, with a flick of her fingers, her magic slid over the wound. The skin knitted back together as if nothing had touched it at all.

Nothing… except him.

Raveena kept her gaze on the reflection in the mirror, letting herself drink Graham in the way her pride wouldn't allow directly. He was taller than she remembered. Broader. His coat was dusted with snow and stable grit, his shoulders squared like a man who bore too many burdens for too long.

He wasn't symmetrical. He never had been. One eye a fraction larger than the other. His nose too prominent, slightly crooked from a break that hadn't healed cleanly. His top lip was thinner than the full, expressive bottom one. And that beard—it was wild, a little too long, a little too coarse.

But gods, he was still him. Still the one man who never tried to conquer her, only to match her. Still the only one she hadn't been able to forget.

"You look tired," she said softly, her fingers brushing the rim of a crystal perfume bottle.

He didn't answer. Just stood there in the center of her chambers, dagger still in hand. He looked at the weapon, accusation in his gaze. He reached for his side and, with a curse, sheathed the blade.

Raveena forgot about Charming. Forgot about Snow. Forgot about the crown and the court and the game she'd been playing with cutthroat queens and fickle princes. Forgot the castle, even—the thing she claimed to love most.

Because he was here. And when Graham was here, there was no room for anything else. He'd always done that to her. Always made the rest of the world fall away.

With Graham, she could close her eyes and not watch her back. She could breathe without planning her next move. She could put down her burdens—the crown, the expectations, the ice that curled tightly around her chest—and rest in the warmth of him.

Graham knew what she needed without asking. Knew how to touch her like he was reading a map only he had memorized. She didn't have to command, didn't have to beg. Though he would make her.

And gods, she wanted him to make her beg. He was the only person she was happy to go to her knees for.

She turned from the mirror. The weight of his gaze wrapped around her like a chain. Slowly, deliberately, she gathered the hem of her velvet gown. With her fingertips, she lifted it up, inch by inch, revealing the pale skin of her thighs. Just as she was about to bend the knee, Graham shifted.

His eyes darkened. Suspicion flashed like a storm cloud. Raveena saw the flicker in his jaw, the tension rolling down his arms. And then—rage.

He moved.

Not like a man possessed by lust. He moved like a lover, consumed by fury. He prowled toward her in three sharp strides, yanked the fabric up with rough hands—hands she'd once worshipped—and stared down at the flesh between her thighs.

His breath hitched. His face turned murderous. "Who did that to you?"

It wasn't until she followed his gaze that she remembered. The bruise. A shadow blooming violet on the soft inner part of her thigh. A careless grip, a pleasure-less moment she hadn't thought twice about.

"It's nothing," she said, but the words were brittle.

Graham's hand hovered over the mark, trembling. Not from desire. From restraint.

"You call that nothing?" he hissed.

"You've given me worse bruises."

"Only after I made you forget your name and then pass out from pleasure."

Raveena waggled her head at the truth of those words.

"It was one of the princelings. Charming, I'm guessing."

Raveena shrugged noncommittally instead of confirming it.

"Either he's an inexperienced child or an inconsiderate twat. Or both, I'm assuming."

She twisted her lips. Charming was both. An expert lover like Graham would know.

"I'm guessing he didn't make you come."

Again, she didn't answer. She didn't need to. Graham would know.

"Bastard. I'll tie his dick in a knot."

Raveena smiled then. She rarely saw the jealous side of Graham. The man knew that no one could turn her inside out like he did. He'd warned her about that, and he'd had the right of it.

She hadn't had a proper orgasm in three years. Certainly not in her husband's bed where he preferred she lie back and think of Thornhall. Actually, that was exactly what she thought of when the old man had done his royal duty atop her.

When Charming had been atop her, he had only been concerned for his own pleasure. Raveena doubted the prince knew that a woman's body could grip a man's cock in a way to heighten their own release. He hadn't given her enough time to show him with his singular performance. She really didn't want to go back for a repeat show. But she would have to if she wanted to keep this castle.

And she would keep this castle.

Now that Graham was back, this time, she would keep him as well.

"Goddess, I missed you. The look of you. The feel of you. The smell of you." Raveena wrinkled her nose. He smelled of horse. "You didn't wash before coming to me?"

Graham flinched, just slightly, the corner of his mouth twitching with memory.

Raveena wasn't trying to wound him with an insult. She was trying to pull him back into her bed. Maybe they'd share a bath first. They could fuck in the bath. In the perfumed depths of the waters, she would remind him that she belonged to no one but him. That she'd only ever surrendered herself to him.

They stood there, inches apart. The hem of her gown tangled in his fists. Her skin was bare and burning. His jaw clenched like he was holding back a scream —or a kiss.

"I didn't come to fuck you, Raveena."

"Then what? To kill me?" She looked down at the dagger.

"I should. Turnabout is fair play."

"I did not send you to war." It was an old argument. One she did not want to revisit, not when they could be tangling in the sheets. It had been three long years.

"You might as well have. What other choice did I have?"

"You could've stayed."

"And been your lover."

"Yes."

"I told you, I don't share. I won't share you. Ever."

"My husband is dead."

"Yet you're jockeying for a newer model."

"Because I failed with the first to produce an heiress."

Graham's nostrils flared. He bared his teeth like a wolf ready to go in for the kill. That had been the worst of their arguments, the thought that another man would get her with child. With a harsh growl, he turned away from her.

Raveena reached for his chin and got a handful of beard. It was softer than she'd suspected. She turned his head back to face her. "Put your babe in my belly. I'll marry Charming. Then I'll kill him. And we can live happily ever after."

"You'd do that? You'd take a man's life?"

"How many lives have you taken these last three years?"

"I was at war."

"So am I."

CHAPTER SIX

She was a queen. This was how they thought. The lives of men meant nothing to them. Males were all pawns on the game board as far as any snow queen was concerned.

Graham looked again at the spot on her neck where his dagger had pierced. He'd felt the break of her skin viscerally. But not as deep as he'd felt that bruise on her inner thigh.

There had been nights he'd envisioned her head on a platter. But when he zoomed out in those dreams, the rest of her body was also on a serving tray. Naked. For him to feast upon.

He would never be able to kill her. This had been a fool's errand. This woman held him by the heart just as much as she held him by the balls.

"I won't kill your prince for you, Raveena."

"Fine. Then kill the princess."

Graham pinched the bridge of his nose. It was the second time tonight he'd been tasked with killing a royal. He'd barely been back in the city for a full day and already the intrigues were trying to drown him. All he wanted was to return to his pint of ale. Get sloshed. Then sleep it off for a week.

No, that wasn't entirely true. What he truly wanted was a taste between this woman's thighs. He wanted to erase that bruise that the fool had left her and bury her with pleasure that only he could give her as that sweet nectar ran down her thighs.

That was the drink he needed. That was the stupor he wanted to drown himself in. He'd left this place to get lost when the only place he'd ever truly been able to lose himself was inside of her.

"Take off your dress, Raveena."

The queen's grin was triumphant at the command.

Graham watched her disrobe. Watched the reveal of the pale skin that was white as snow. The curtain of the gown lifted on the rosebud of a nipple that he knew could go blood red if he pinched it hard enough. The petals of her labia that he'd suckle until that flower was engorged.

"Lie back on the bed and spread your thighs."

She did as she was told. This queen of the realm was

completely bare, completely defenseless against him. No, that was never true either.

She had magic that could turn him cold. She had never used it on him. Would never need to. She knew she held his will in the palm of her hand.

Though if that were true, she wouldn't have allowed him to leave her. She would've made him stay. She would have forced him to sneak into her bed each night after the king consort left her.

Would that have been so bad? He knew the old man hadn't had her heart. Knew she hadn't had his. King White had loved his first wife. A rare love match in this matriarchal kingdom where women traded men as bed partners all the time.

Raveena had had lovers before him. But she'd had none since they found each other. Graham knew that for a fact. Had never once questioned it. Which was why he was so floored when she'd accepted the king's hand in marriage.

That vow that Raveena gave King Snow of her own free will had hurt Graham more than if she had cheated on him.

Graham took her hand now. He brought her fingertips to his lips. He pressed a gentle kiss to her index finger, then her thumb. His lips trailed a path to her palm. There, he tasted the salt of her skin. It was just as he remembered. Her taste hadn't changed.

It was as though someone turned the lights on inside of him. All of the memories of their time together came flooding back in the vivid color of spring—lush and blinding and impossible to ignore.

He remembered the first time he'd seen her, high above the training yard, sunlight kissing the silver-threaded braid that crowned her pale hair. He'd been bloodied from a sparring match, chest heaving, sweat in his eyes, and yet she'd made the whole world still. Princess Raveena of Fenvalen, perched like a queen-in-waiting on the stone balcony, had looked down at him as if he were something worthy of notice. That look alone had undone him more than any blade ever had.

Graham had never liked getting tangled with royal women. They wanted things—discretion, power, pleasure without consequence. He preferred the blunt honesty of village girls who knew what it meant to share a bed and a burden.

He told himself he'd only take a taste. Raveena had tasted like fire and frost. After the first time, he hadn't been able to stop. She'd pulled him back night after night, eyes burning, magic clinging to her skin, whispering secrets against his neck like spells that would never break.

They had made a world in the shadows of Fenvalen's stone towers. A world of warm beds and whispered promises and the kind of love that left marks no one could see. Oh, he'd marked her milk-white thighs, to be sure. She'd hidden them beneath corsets and lace, only the two of them knowing they were there.

Graham had started to believe it might last. That maybe he wasn't just her distraction. Then the courtship by their nearest ally. Then the engagement. Then her wedding night when she took another man into her bed after he'd made her thighs shake and tears threaten her eyes.

Now in that same bedroom where he'd last had his princess, Graham pulled the queen's hand from his mouth. He placed her hand on her thigh. "Heal it."

Raveena searched his eyes. All she got back was his hard, implacable glare. She did as she was told.

Ice prickled at his fingertips as her magic came forth. When she pulled her hand away, it was as though the bruise had never been there. If only Graham could erase Charming's touch from her mind. If only he could be the prince to give his queen what she truly needed. Instead, he gave her what she wanted.

Graham spread Raveena's thighs wide. He looked over the flesh that wept for him: pale pink, blushing red with the heated desire that pooled there.

"I'm not going to kill your stepdaughter, Ray."

"Fine. Throw her in the dungeons."

"And the prince?"

"Like I said, after we marry and I'm with child, we throw him in the dungeons as well."

"Open yourself to me."

Raveena placed her hands on either side of her labia. With her fingertips, she pulled the flushed flesh apart. Her body undulated under his perusal, eager.

"These are all things *you* want." Graham rested his head against her thigh as he looked at his favorite sight in all the world. "What do *I* get out of it?"

"You get me."

Graham's teeth flashed—white and sharp like the wolves that prowled the ice-laced forests of Fenvalen. That old, familiar hunger coiled low in his gut, the kind he thought he'd buried on the battlefield but never quite shook—not where she was concerned.

"Hmm." The sound rumbled in his throat like a satisfied growl. "You're right, Ray. I do want you. Badly."

He didn't wait for permission. He never had—not with her. His head dipped, and he sank his teeth into the soft curve at the apex of her thigh, claiming her the way beasts claimed what was theirs. Not to hurt. Not to wound. But to mark. To remind her—and anyone who dared come near her—that this thing between them had never burned out. It had smoldered, banked beneath years and war and betrayal, but now it roared to life again.

Raveena arched toward him. Her clit grew bigger, rounder with each nip of his teeth. He hadn't even touched her there. Her skin still tasted of snowmelt and summer lightning.

"I want something more than my queen's attentions."

"Anything. Name it."

He held her gaze. Didn't blink. "I want Greymoor."

Even though her body pooled with pleasure, Graham felt the calculation in her mind. Saw it in the curl of her fingers. "Greymoor? You're asking for territory I've been negotiating with the Winter Assembly over?"

The land was on the eastern border. It lay between Everfrost and Fenvalen and shared a slight border with Valebright, the Charming stronghold. The tract was near the river mouth, where the spruce trees grew thick and wild. Because it bordered three queendoms, no one ruled there. There his men could be free of anyone's rule, save their own.

Her hesitation made him want it all the more. The fact that she was thinking it over, considering his ask, made him giddy. He knew all the right buttons to push, and so he did.

"You're the queen. Get it for me and I'll take care of your little problem."

He tapped her clit. She snapped her legs closed,

trying to hold his hand in place so she could receive her pleasure. But he was already pulling away from her and striding toward the door.

"Graham!"

Graham paused at the door and called over his shoulder, "If you let him touch you again, I will castrate him, and the deal is off."

And with that, he walked out.

CHAPTER SEVEN

Raveena's steps were deliberate, her gait slowed by the weight of her own body. This morning, she'd had a thigh gap; that space between a woman's inner thighs when she stands with her feet together. Though the majority of the queens in the Snow Kingdom wore long gowns that covered their entire bodies, when they disrobed in saunas or indoor pools, they all displayed that particular stance on beauty that indicated that they were youthful and thin. After her encounter with Graham, Raveena would not be showcasing that particular fad anytime soon.

The space between her thighs was no longer bruised. It was swollen. Graham had left his mark with the deep, unshakable ache of being thoroughly claimed but not quite satisfied. Her inner muscles fluttered with every step, sore from pleasure, from surrender. She should have drawn herself a bath. Should have curled beneath velvet sheets and let the warmth coax the tension from her limbs. But she was a queen. So she walked on—wearing the evidence of him like a secret crown.

It was cruel, the way he played with her. Always had been. He'd wind her up until she was coiled like a spring, trembling on the edge of release, only to pull away—just to hear her beg. Just to see if she would.

She always did.

And by the godmothers, she would again. Only the next time, she would have him fully, forever. She would tether him to this place like the walls tethered her—firm, inescapable, hers.

Her fingers drifted along the brickwork as she passed, gliding over the cool surface of the stones. The palace hummed around her, solid and familiar. The fixtures, the sconces, the etched frost-glass panes. Every curve and corner of this castle held her shape. She had poured herself into it over the years—into its defenses, its traditions, its elegance. It had become an extension of her body, of her rule, of her strength.

It protected her.

It obeyed her.

It stayed.

Just like Graham would.

There would be no more wars. Raveena had spoken peace into being with the other kingdoms. Sliced through politics with the same precision she used to carve an adversary's ambition to pieces. No more battlefields. No more months spent watching for Graham's name to appear on a casualty list.

The Snow Kingdom had sent nothing to aid the other kingdoms when the trolls first descended from the mountains—no soldiers, no steel, not even a single sack of grain. Not until Graham had volunteered the day after she said her vows to another man. The next day, she'd set to work.

Behind closed doors and beneath layers of diplomacy, Raveena had done what kings could not: forged quiet alliances, mended old grudges, and stirred pride from dusty matriarchies. She had promised them security, trade, and shared defense. In her heart, all of it had to ensure that one man came home.

One ally, however, came at a sharper price.

Valebright. The Charmings had extended olive branches through gilded letters and velvet-wrapped envoys. They had offered Raveena the backing of their coffers and court—provided her stepdaughter was made available for their young prince to court. It had seemed a tidy solution. Snow White, always playing at sweetness, would be safely delivered into another queen's hands. The union would elevate her, move her out of Thornhall, and solidify Raveena's claim as the ruling queen without bloodshed.

Then the king had died and left Snow with the stronger claim to Thornhall. The Charmings had begun to circle like vultures cloaked in velvet. Raveena's plans had to shift again. If she claimed the prince, she might lose her hunter.

She crossed the courtyard and descended the narrow path to the stables. The scent of hay and horses thickened with every step—earthy, warm, tinged with leather and snow. The stables smelled like him. She heard echoes of his laughter bouncing off the wooden walls. She caught a shadow of him pressing her against the walls, the stall doors—wherever he could get her alone.

Raveena smiled as she reached the entrance. The wintry evening air was crisp and sharp against her skin. Her blood was already singing. But when she stepped inside, her smile vanished.

Snow White stood in the center of the stables. Light sliced through the beams above, catching on her raven black hair. She was brushing down a chestnut mare with quiet focus. Her gloves were off. Her delicate hands moved in slow, practiced strokes.

Snow looked up at the sound of Raveena's entrance, blinking once. That ever-serene smile touched her lips. It was the same one she'd used since girlhood, soft and unassuming, like a blade disguised as a blossom.

"Stepmother," she said, tone honeyed with deference.

Raveena's lips curved, but it wasn't a smile. "Why aren't you attending to our guests?"

"I needed some air." Snow set down the brush, then gently stroked the mare's neck. "The court is so… thick with perfume and politics. The horses are simpler. They never lie."

Horses shifted in their stalls. The occasional stomp of a hoof or flick of a tail was the only interruption in the silence that stretched between the two women.

"Except Charming." Snow ducked her head, but her smile lifted so high her cheeks were nearly in her ears. "He's been so attentive since he returned. Even more than before. It's as though something's changed in him. As if he knows what he wants now."

Oh, the boy knew what he wanted. In bed, at least. And that was just to please himself. Raveena remembered his hands fumbling at her waist, his mouth trailing wet heat down her skin without finesse, his breath panting her name like it was a prize he hadn't earned. She'd lain still beneath him, eyes on the ceiling, counting the seconds between his desperation and his release. He'd found his pleasure quickly, selfishly, as boys often did.

Outside the bedroom, the princeling needed a woman's strong touch. Just like all noble men did. It's why the matriarchs had taken possession of all crowns across the snow-covered lands generations ago.

"He has been decisive of late," Raveena said smoothly. "He told me he had no doubts left. That he'd never felt so… consumed."

Snow blinked. "Consumed?"

"Mmm." Raveena plucked a strand of straw from her sleeve and dropped it. "He said he needed someone who could understand him. Match his fire. Someone experienced enough not to be afraid of what he is."

And yet as the words left her tongue, her mind strayed—not to Charming. To Graham. To the burn of his eyes, the sound of his voice like gravel and thunder. The way he growled when she dared touch what he called his. The way he looked at her—not with lust or reverence—but ownership. Graham didn't worship her. He claimed her.

If you let him touch you again, I will castrate him.

Raveena pressed her thighs together at the memory. Her swollen flesh thrummed to life. Her clit pulsed, still eager for the orgasm Graham had denied her. She hadn't bothered to get herself off. She'd been doing that for the last three years and had never once reached the teeth-chattering, soul-shaking orgasm that only Graham could give her.

No, she'd bide her time and wait for her hunter's bite. Because he would come back to her. He was angry now, but he must know the truth. He must have known that no man had ever meant anything to her. Not since him. Not before him. Not the old man she'd married. Not the boy she'd seduced.

Charming was a pawn. A stepping stone to the crown she would never surrender, the castle that felt more like a lover than most men she'd known. Once she secured her position—once a daughter grew safe and sound in her womb—Charming would become expendable. A necessary casualty.

"And when the prince proposes," Raveena said, voice light as frost, "what will you say?"

Snow smiled with teeth now. "Why, yes, of course. As any queen would."

Raveena stepped closer, close enough to smell the floral oil in Snow's hair. She refused to let the fragrance wrinkle her nose. "Remember what I taught you; prepare for surprises, my dear."

The two women held each other's gaze—neither blinking, neither backing down. Around them, the stable fell to silence. Both believed they'd won. Both believed they were the one Charming would choose.

Raveena turned first, her cloak snapping behind her

like a banner of storm clouds, the scent of her magic sharp in the air. She didn't look back as she left the stables.

She didn't need to. The game was in play, and she was certain she'd already won.

CHAPTER EIGHT

Graham stepped out of the stall with the slow, silent ease of a man who'd spent too long in other people's shadows. Once again, straw clung to his coat. The scent of horses and leather curled thick in his nose. Cold air licked at the back of his neck. It was nothing compared to the fire crawling just beneath his skin.

He watched Raveena walk away through the open stable doors, the sway of her hips a practiced weapon. But it wasn't the sway that held his gaze—it was the slight stumble in her step. Barely there. The smallest hitch. But he saw it.

That hitch in her gait, that was him. His doing. His touch, his mouth, his refusal. Her body was still singing with need, still craving what he had denied her. He knew the signs; he'd spent years learning them. Raveena didn't stumble unless someone had gotten under her skin. He was the only one who had ever managed to do it.

Just like he saw the tension in her shoulders, the way her spine held too straight, too proud—like armor polished to hide the cracks. Her gown clung to her like smoke and snow, the silver embroidery catching the fading light, casting flickers of frost across the stone walls as she moved. She wore elegance like a blade, beauty like a challenge. A queen through and through.

He also saw the softness beneath it all. He knew the taste of it, the texture of it. His flesh knew the tremble of her breath against his neck, the desperate clutch of her fingers in his hair, the way her body would melt under his.

That softness was his. Had been, once. Still was, he thought, with a wolf's certainty that didn't care for courtly games or royal arrangements.

But now she was offering it to a prince in order to keep a crown. They'd been here before. Had this exact same argument that had split them apart.

She hadn't changed. She was playing politics again. Making bargains with men who wore crowns they hadn't earned. Betraying him—not with love, not with lust, but with strategy.

Graham should have hated her for it. Instead, he

burned. Because even when she was scheming and lying and handing off her body, he knew he had her heart. Sluggish, cold, dark thing that it was. It belonged to her, but she had given it to him.

He didn't doubt she would discard the prince after she got what she wanted. He was still unclear what exactly had happened to end the last king of Thornhall. Graham supposed that's why the princess had sought him out upon his return.

He still wanted to tear down every banner in Thornhall and claim Raveena like he'd claimed her body. Still wanted to crawl beneath the thorny façade and find the wild girl from Fenvalen who had whispered his name in the dark.

But she was walking away. Again. And he wasn't sure if he wanted to follow her… or drag her back.

"I see you had trouble the first time I asked you to kill her."

Graham said nothing. His silence was an answer in itself.

"Do you think you can follow through now? After hearing how little you matter to her?"

Graham stared at the princess. Little Snow White had grown up in these last few years. The soft-faced girl with pigtails and ribbons was gone. In her place stood a woman who could gut a man with her words and bury him with her smile.

She was cold. Clean. Calculated.

She reminded him—far too much—of her stepmother.

He wasn't sure whether that was Raveena's doing or something deeper in Snow's bloodline. He doubted ruthlessness could be taught. But maybe it could be caught, like frostbite.

Graham moved away from the stall where he'd hid at Raveena's approach. He had felt her arrival before he saw her—before the sound of her boots crunched over the snow-packed ground, before her silhouette appeared in the stable's shadowed archway.

Some instinct always alerted him when she was near. A shift in the wind. The flap of a moth's wing in a new direction. The fall of a snowflake that melted when it hit the ground. He was attuned to her in a way that went deeper than logic, older than memory. Just as the women of Everfrost were said to have ice in their veins, the men of Fenvalen were said to carry the blood of wolves.

Graham had scented his fated mate the moment he first laid eyes on Raveena. Had known it for a fact the first time he'd tasted her. Had erased all doubts the second her inner muscles had grasped his cock in an orgasmic chokehold. He belonged to her, and gods help him, she belonged to him.

Except she didn't see it that way. Raveena wanted a

throne beneath her and a crown above. Graham only wanted her hand in his. Right now, he crossed the distance to her stepdaughter, preparing to engage in a plot to thwart those efforts.

"She still thinks she'll win," he said.

Snow's lips curved faintly. "She always does. She thought she'd keep this castle after she murdered my father."

Graham made a noncommittal sound at the princess's accusation. It wasn't that he didn't put murder beneath his queen. He knew she was capable. He just couldn't puzzle out how murdering the king before securing a place outside this castle for his daughter would win Raveena what she truly prized.

He let his gaze wander back to the open stable doors. Raveena's scent still lingered in the air—snow lilies, frost, and that warm spice that only rose when her blood was up. He'd had his head between her thighs not long ago, breathing her in as he debated whether or not to slit her throat.

If she did go through with marrying that weak-jawed excuse for a prince—if she let Charming touch her again — Well, then Graham might just have to honor the deal he'd made with the snow princess.

His voice was low when he finally spoke. "I'll do what needs to be done, Your Highness."

CHAPTER NINE

The bells rang cold through the corridor. Three chimes, crisp and sharp as chisel strikes. Parliament was in session.

Raveena swept through the palace with the composure of an avalanche contained in crystal. Her gown was a tailored marvel of midnight velvet, the hem frosted with embroidered silver thorns. A crown of jet and ice nestled in her hair, gleaming like the edges of a well-honed blade. She moved without hurry, her steps a study in control. Every heel-click on the marble was an assertion: *I am still queen.*

The doors to the Frost Hall opened before her. Arctic air rushed to greet her like an old friend. The scent of frost permeated the hall with a faint, metallic layer of ozone. High above, icicle chandeliers caught and fractured the light into frozen rainbows. The chamber held the White Table, carved from a single slab of glacier-stone, gleaming and cold enough to sting bare skin. Around it sat the House of Ladies, the ruling body of the Snow Kingdom—nobles, generals, mistresses of coin and trade, queens without thrones, and queens who had made thrones out of bone.

Raveena took her place at the northmost arc of the table. Her seat was taller, darker, less decorative than the rest. Just how she liked it.

The day's docket unraveled in the hands of the Lady Archivist. Her gloved fingers were steady as she smoothed the parchment across the long obsidian table. Trade routes to reopen, grain stores to redistribute. Merchant guilds pressing for winter tariffs to be lifted now that the Troll Wars had ended. The archivist's voice, calm and clipped, carried over the flickering hush of the chamber.

The conversation soon curled into arguments as the ladies debated treaties and alliances, their jeweled hands gesturing sharply in the firelight. Old grudges resurfaced like thawed beasts. Every proposed accord was met with pointed suspicion or gilded derision.

"The Eastern Reaches are vulnerable," said Lady Hollowmere, fingers drumming her cup. "If we do not reestablish trade, we risk losing influence entirely."

"They grow nothing of value," said Lady Veyne. "Better to let them beg."

A murmur of agreement rippled. Across the table, Lady Tern raised her voice over the clamor. "What of the Forest Kingdom? And the Coastal Kingdom? They held the line when the trolls broke through."

"Both ruled by fresh blood," someone scoffed. "Those two boys are barely crowned and already seeking our approval."

Raveena spoke then, her voice slicing clean through the room. "Which is precisely why we should consider alliances with King Phillip and King Eric. I'm hearing good things about their brides, Queen Maleficent and Queen Ursula. Queens who rise through fire are often far more capable than kings who inherit through birthright."

A hush followed, wary but attentive. Each woman was wise enough to hold her peace as they watched how the game of the Thornhall throne played out.

Raveena steepled her fingers. "The Forest Queen is young, yes, but she held her borders while we bled on ours. I hear the Coastal Queen dismantled her brother's maritime council before the first session."

That brought a titter of praise from the room of bloodthirsty noble ladies gathered. Though each held their pieces close to their chests, they could admire another woman's gameplay from afar. Especially when her moves crushed an entire patriarchal society.

"I do not care if they are newly throned. I care that they understand power and how to wield it."

Lady Charming made a soft, disdainful chirp at this.

Raveena turned her gaze on her with all the cold grace of a glacier shifting toward ruin. "You have thoughts you'd like to share with the group, Lady Charming?"

The older woman's smile was brittle. "Only that it's a bold position for someone whose seat is... shall we say... temporarily occupied. With your stepdaughter's impending marriage, I wonder how much longer your voice will carry weight in this chamber."

Ah. There it was. The blood-scent beneath the perfume.

"Impending marriage, you say? That's curious. I hadn't heard of any proposal." Raveena glanced at her nails. The same nails that had made half-moons in Prince Charming's back. The same nails she wouldn't hesitate to stab into Lady Charming's back if the woman kept interfering with her plans. "Though I had heard a rather intriguing rumor—something about Prince Charming seen sneaking back to his chambers last night... from the opposite direction of my step-daughter's rooms."

A ripple of muffled laughter and thinly veiled coughs moved around the White Table.

Lady Charming's knuckles whitened on the rim of her goblet. Her smile tightened, brittle as ice at the center of a deep, still pool—the kind that only looked calm until it cracks beneath the weight of something heavier than pride. The plum silk of her bodice rose and fell with a breath drawn too carefully, too slowly. Only the flare of her nostrils betrayed the fury coiled beneath her jeweled composure.

She lifted her chin a fraction—imperious, unbowed. Her eyes glittered with the calculation of a hawk denied its prey.

Raveena snorted. The one thing she would never be accused of was being prey. "Perhaps the prince has found his appetites… elsewhere."

Lady Charming's face darkened like a sky before a snowstorm, but she said nothing.

Raveena turned her attention back to the table, her voice smooth as glass. "The Troll Wars are over. This kingdom cannot thrive on tradition or outdated alliances. We must surge forward on strategy—and on the company we choose to keep."

She let her words hang in the cold air like icicles ready to drop. She was still queen, and she had no plans to relinquish her crown. Especially if her stepdaughter's crown just so happened to fall off her severed head.

Raveena knew Graham would not let her down. Well, not outside of a withheld orgasm. But even that was temporary. The huntsman always paid his debts in the bedroom. She couldn't wait until their next match.

"There's one more matter I'd like to raise before we adjourn."

Goblets lowered. Chairs shifted. Quills stilled. A few glances flicked toward her, waiting for her to continue. Some glances were curious. Most were wary.

"The parcel of land on the southern ridge," Raveena continued. "Near the glacial run where the ice thaws early. It was previously earmarked for a diplomatic retreat, if I recall correctly."

"You mean Greymoor?" Lady Tern frowned, flipping through her notes. "The site slated for the Unity Lodge?"

"The same." Raveena folded her hands atop the stone. "I'd like to reclaim it. Repossess it in the crown's name. The Unity Lodge can be relocated."

"Relocated where, Your Majesty?" asked Lady Veyne, a sharpness beneath her courtesy.

Raveena smiled faintly. "Somewhere less… central. Less scenic. Surely peace doesn't require such a view."

Lady Hollowmere cleared her throat. "Forgive me, but that land was donated to the Assembly by the Icebound Guild for the sole purpose of diplomatic hospitality. To revoke it now would risk more than paperwork."

Lady Charming leaned forward, eyes glittering like icicles catching blood. "One might almost think you've made promises that require payment."

Raveena's spine stayed straight, her lips curved in a smile too perfect to be kind. "One might think a queen need not explain her decisions to a body she carried through a war."

The table bristled—not openly, not yet. But she felt it. A shift beneath the calm. Small fractures forming in the ice.

Raveena tilted her head, looking down the long curve of the White Table. They'd liked her talk of alliances. They'd liked her jabs at Lady Charming and the subtle reminder of her continued power. But this land? Greymoor? This appeared a more touchy subject than she'd suspected.

Graham wanted the land. He'd bled for this kingdom. Sacrificed everything. Well, not everything. She would have never allowed anything or anyone to take his life. Behind the scenes, she'd shifted orders around, overrode generals' calls, and repositioned the pieces on the game board to ensure that her lover could fight— yes—but would largely remain unharmed.

All he'd asked in return was for Greymoor. And for her not to fuck Charming. That was doable. But she'd still have to marry the boy. Graham would have to get over that. To help him get over it, she would hand him this land.

The House of Ladies' polished nails and paper-thin smiles stood in her way. Though not for long. This would not be easy. She would have to push. She would have to fight. But this game was child's play. She would win with one hand tied behind her back.

Thinking of knots and bound hands made her think of Graham and how he could make her beg. He was the only person she'd ever begged for anything. Because he gave her everything.

She would not beg these women. She would make them bleed if they got in her way.

CHAPTER TEN

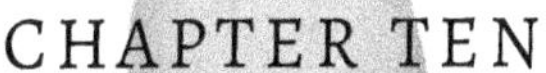

The castle loomed behind him. Its spires caught the morning light like the points of a crown carved from ice. Graham didn't look back.

He never did.

His boots crunched through fresh frost as he walked the path beyond the gates, shoulders hunched against the bite of the wind. The air out here was sharp and clean, laced with wood smoke and the faint metallic scent of snow-soaked iron. He inhaled deep, letting it fill his lungs. Clean air. Honest air.

It didn't erase the stink of palace politics that clung to him. Or the taste of her name sitting heavy on his tongue.

Raveena.

Gods, he'd done this walk too many times, the walk

of shame. It had never felt shameful in their youth. He'd felt pride at being her chosen lover. Honored at being her confidant. Triumph believing he held her heart in his hand.

That last part had been a lie. She'd chosen him. She'd confided in him. But she had not given him her heart. Her body, yes. But he wanted—no, needed—more than that.

And so this walk away from the castle with empty hands and a sluggish heart came with footsteps weighted down by shame.

Once again, out he went. Through the castle gates, down into the village with sweat cooling on his skin and bruises hidden beneath the collar of his coat. Not all the bruises had been from her touch. Sometimes they came from wanting her. From believing she was his.

It hadn't always been about the bed. Often, it hadn't been about the bed at all. Some nights, they'd spent hours side by side, her legs draped across his lap while they played strategy games with carved bone pieces and rules they rewrote as they went. Other times, she'd read aloud from some ancient text while he listened, pointing out the cracks in the histories with a soldier's pragmatism and a mind built for attack.

Graham had never had a formal education. He hadn't needed one. His brilliance lived in battlefield instinct, in angles and pressure points, in knowing when to strike and when to wait.

Raveena saw that intelligence. She admired it. He could match her wit for wit. He'd thought she saw him not just as a man, but as her man.

Fated mates.

Graham scoffed, dragging a hand through his hair. How stupid he'd been.

She was a queen. He was just a man. Not even a prince. Not even close.

The village stirred around him as he reached its edge. Smoke curled from the chimneys. Market stalls were being set up for the day, their awnings snapping in the wind. Children darted through slush-patched streets, their laughter a sharp contrast to the noise in his head.

Graham cut across the square and headed toward the old barracks. It wasn't much—a few repurposed buildings on the outer edge of town. It was where the soldiers who survived the Troll Wars had been quartered. His men. His brothers. The ones who'd bled beside him in the dirt and snow.

The land was hard here. Rocky, uneven, half-frozen most of the year. Nothing grew right. Not like in Fenvalen. He couldn't go back there. The past was buried under too much snow and blood.

Greymoor was the next best thing. It had give.

Beneath the frost and pine, the earth held promise. He'd walked the ridge lines, tested the soil with his own hands. Things could grow there—barley, root vegetables, maybe even fruit trees with enough tending. It was land that didn't demand blood for its loyalty, only sweat. That was a bargain Graham understood.

More than that, it was quiet. Remote enough to slip under the queens' watchful gazes. Close enough that if Raveena ever needed him, he could be there before nightfall.

No courts. No crowns. No games played with daughters and dowries. Just land. Men and women side by side, building something worth passing down. A different kind of kingdom. One not ruled but lived in.

Raveena had promised it to him for the price of Snow White's head.

Snow had promised him the same boon for the same price.

Graham stared out at the gray fields, jaw tight. If either woman made good on their word, he and his men could build something that lasted. Not just barracks but homes. A future.

But which of them would keep her word?

Raveena—the woman who ruled with silk and steel, who seduced with her eyes and lied with her silence? The one who made him feel like a king one minute and a fool the next?

Or Snow—the girl with ice in her veins and fire behind her smile, who wore innocence like armor and had the gall to command his loyalty like it was her birthright?

One offered him passion, the other purpose.

One knew him in every intimate way and still chose power over him. The other needed him—not for his body but his sword, his name, his fury.

Two women.

Two promises.

One future.

And not a damn bit of trust left in him.

Graham turned away from the land, from the barracks, from the castle looming in the distance. The snow was falling again—soft, quiet, relentless. Just like fate.

He didn't know which queen would win this war of wits. But he knew he wouldn't lose again.

The barracks smelled like smoke and steel and men who'd fought too long in the cold. The scent hit Graham the moment he opened the door—sweat, leather, the charred meat someone had been roasting over a barrel of fire in the far corner. It was a welcome smell, grounding in a way the perfume-choked halls of the castle could never be. Here, the air was honest. Here, no one pretended to be something they weren't.

The men looked up as he stepped inside. A chorus of laughter and hoarse shouts erupted around the room.

"Well, look who finally remembered he's one of us."

"Graham the Ghost returns."

"Thought you'd defected to royal service. Or royal bedchambers."

Graham gave a tired grunt of acknowledgment as a few of them rose to clasp arms with him. Their grips were hard, familiar. Real. These were the brothers he'd bled beside in the snow, men who'd held the line when the world threatened to fall in.

"You missed the parade," said Corwin. The red-bearded giant had soot on his cheeks and a grin full of mischief. "Should've seen it. The noble ladies were out in full frost. More than one winked at me."

"Or maybe they had a tic?" said Lars, a thin reed of a man who was wicked with a bow and arrow. "Or they were drunk."

"Very drunk," Corwin agreed with a satisfied grunt.

Graham smirked, but it didn't reach his eyes.

"You weren't with us," Corwin continued, narrowing his gaze. "Which means you were either in the castle... or in the queen."

A round of rough laughter followed. No one even pretended to whisper. The affair between Graham and Raveena had never been a secret. In the Snow Kingdom, noblewomen bedded who they pleased. Love was fleeting, loyalty negotiable. But marriage—that was something else entirely.

Women only married princes. Men with armies. Men with land. Men with crowns to be seized and power to be folded into the snow-laced branches of her lineage. Men who could be used.

Graham? He was a good way to pass the night. A warm mouth, a stronger hand. A moment's pleasure.

"The Winter Games are starting soon," said one of the younger soldiers as he sharpened a blade by the fire. "First time in years we've made it back in time to compete."

"Be good to put my axe to something that doesn't scream," someone muttered.

"You going to join the games, Graham?" Corwin asked, tossing him a flask. "Or are you too busy climbing up royal skirts?"

Graham caught the flask and took a long sip. The mead burned sweet and sharp down his throat. "I'll think on it."

He had more pressing matters to plan. Not one, but two murders danced at the edge of his thoughts. Raveena's if she married Charming. Charming if he stood in Graham's way of getting Raveena back. Snow if she demanded his loyalty over his heart.

"So," another voice piped up, "everyone's saying

Charming will propose during the Assembly. Big royal spectacle. Kiss in the snow. Real heartstring shit."

"Then what?" Corwin asked. "Queen Raveena's out of a crown. What's she going to do without a throne?"

The question silenced the laughter. Everyone turned to Graham. Graham didn't answer.

It was something he hadn't considered. Raveena without a crown on her head? What if it was gone and she had no kingdom left to rule, no reason to chase power or bind herself to a prince?

What if she looked up and finally saw—him? No throne. No pawns. Just him.

Maybe then she would come away with Graham. To the land she'd promised him if he took care of her snowy problem. He could build something for her, something lasting.

Maybe she could be his. Really his.

Maybe he didn't need to kill anyone.

Maybe he just needed to remove the crown out of their way.

Graham took another sip from the flask, slower this time, gaze fixed on the flames licking at the logs in the hearth.

Maybe it was the crown that was her cage. And if he simply knocked it from her head, he'd set her free.

CHAPTER ELEVEN

The flames in the hearth cast long shadows that danced along the frost-veined walls of the bedchamber. Outside, the wind hissed like a stubborn child that would not be put to bed. Within the castle's walls, there was only stillness, the hush of a place held in breath.

Raveena sat at her vanity, cloaked in that silence. The soft whisper of bristles through her hair was the only sound. Each stroke soothed her, steadied her. She had spent the entire day sharpening her mind into a blade. First in the Winter Assembly, parrying threats and dissent with a diplomat's smile, and then in her own court, smoothing over the fractures of a kingdom still healing from war the inhabitants had wanted no part of. A war she'd had no interest in until her lover stormed off with his blade in hand because he needed to cleave through something, or rather someone, and a troll was better than committing regicide.

Today, she had maneuvered every conversation, every glance, every pause to achieve her endgame. Just as she'd done for the last three years to ensure the troll wars ended swiftly with as little blood on the Snow Kingdom's hands as possible. If she'd left the war efforts to the young forest prince, the fighting would still be going on and Graham would still be beyond her reach.

She glanced at the clock on the wall. The hour was late. The minute hand took its time going around the clock's face.

She lowered her brush and exhaled slowly. The silk robe she wore slid open as she shifted. The firelight kissed the line of her collarbone, the dip of her waist, the soft expanse of thigh. Her gaze dropped, and there —just above the bend of her leg—was the mark.

The bite was still red, tender. She bit her lip, regarding the shape of him etched into her flesh. With a fingertip, Raveena traced the edge of the bruise, feeling the ache stir again—not just between her legs but deeper, beneath skin and blood and bone.

She didn't need to look behind her when she heard the movement. The subtle shift of air. The hush of a shadow stepping through darker shadow.

"This one feels lonely." Her fingers brushed the mark. "It needs a companion."

With slow, practiced grace, she opened her robe wide and spread her thighs even wider. The fire in his eyes licked over her skin, gilding her like a statue left for worship.

"You know how symmetry is important to me."

Graham said nothing. But she felt him. Felt the weight of his stare from across the room, from the shadowed corner where he stood—stone-still, silent, radiating heat like a blade held too long over a flame.

His breath was the only giveaway. Just slightly faster than it had been. His body was taut, coiled, waiting.

Raveena dragged her fingers along her inner thigh. Outside, the wind whistled, the chill banging against the window to get in. The heat in the room kept the cold at bay.

Graham's assessing gaze continued to devour her. His stoic silence caused her core to pulse. When his index finger twitched at his side, blood pooled in her clit in anticipation.

"I said," she whispered, voice curling like steam, "I want a matching pair. Would you deny your queen?"

The only movement was a flick of his wrist. Her brain ignored the glint of the blade in his hand. He'd come at her with shackles before and bound her to the bed for his pleasure. He'd tied her limbs in intricate knots that ensured they stayed open for his viewing enjoyment as he made her come so many times that she'd passed out. Breath play was a favorite of hers when he made her gasp while his hand covered her mouth and nose as the other intimate opening gasped around his length.

But knife play? That was new. She was eager to try. She would do anything with Graham. Anything for him. But first he would make her beg. That was her favorite part. Not so much the pleas that burst from her when she finally gave in. The buildup before she gave in. When she tried to hold it in, hold on to her dignity.

Graham never had to snatch the words from her. He never used force. He just had a way of making her want him so much that she would inevitably give in.

Except right now, he wasn't doing anything. He wasn't saying anything. He wasn't making a move. He leaned against the dark oak panels like he was carved from shadow. The firelight danced over him, flickering against the blade he spun idly between his fingers.

Raveena had the patience of a saint. She'd shown that earlier in the throne room as she'd dealt with the queens and ladies. With this man, she had very little chill.

She rose from her vanity in one fluid motion, letting the brush fall to the floor. The hem of her robe whispered along the polished stone as she moved toward him, each step slow and intentional, her bare feet silent against the floor.

Still, he didn't move. Didn't speak. Just let that blade catch the glow of the light and watched her like a predator might watch the flick of a rabbit's ears—patient, practiced, and entirely in control.

"Are you a woman of your word?"

Her smile curled, dark and eager. Ah. A game, then.

"With you?" Her hips swayed with every step that brought her closer to her true endgame. "I have never broken my word."

Graham's scoff was more breath than sound, but it carried enough accusation to cut. "You married another man."

"I gave the king my body," she said, stopping just before him, their breath mingling in the narrow space between them. "Not my heart."

He stared at her—jaw tight, eyes darker than a storm. "Do you even have a heart?"

Raveena's hands went to the straps of her night-gown. She pulled the edges to her shoulders. Along with the robe, the gown slithered off her body, pooling at her bare feet. She inhaled, which pushed her breasts up. The eager nipples throbbed in time to her racing chest.

Instead of looking at her naked body, Graham held her gaze. "Your body belonged to me."

She let her gaze rake over his face—every scar, every shadow, every hard-earned line etched into the man he'd become. The soldier. The ghost. The flame that had never gone out.

"It still does. It's been locked up tight. Waiting for the only man who ever knew what to do with it."

Graham looked then. Looked at the body that had only ever sang for him. The tender flesh of her breasts ached to be close to him. Her knees pressed together, partly to get relief from the pulsing of her core, partly in preparation to launch into him.

The blade stilled in his hand. His chest rose sharply. Heat rolled off him now, barely restrained. Something dark coiled behind his gaze, like a storm behind a dam.

Slowly, deliberately, Raveena sank to her knees before him. Her head lowered, and her hands slid behind her back, fingers lacing together. She tilted her face up to him, her expression not vulnerable but still somehow submissive.

"Take what's yours," she whispered.

Graham swallowed, the column of his throat working while his jaw remained tight. The dagger was still gripped in his callused hand, fingers tightening around the hilt of the blade. He brought the flat edge of the blade under her chin and tilted her face up until her eyes met his.

Dark. Defiant. Drenched in want. Eager to do

anything he asked. Ready to give him anything he asked for.

"I want the land you promised."

Her lips curved, wicked and pleased. "It's yours. I settled it this afternoon. The scrolls are in process. You'll have the deed within the week."

Surprise flickered through him, sharp and swift. He hadn't expected her to follow through. That was odd. She always did exactly what he told her to. After being a brat for a bit because they both enjoyed it.

"Can I have you now?" Her tongue escaped from her mouth, and she licked the flat side of the blade. "It's been so long since I've tasted anything like you. My husband balked the one time I tried."

Graham snatched the dagger away. "Do not speak of other men in your bed, Ray."

"Charming, on the other hand, was very quick on the draw once I got into his pants."

Graham's growl turned feral. "You keep talking, and I swear I'll commit regicide tonight."

Raveena leaned into the crotch of his pants and inhaled that woodsy musk of his. "I only ever found pleasure with you. It's your taste I crave. Always has been. No one else will do."

With those words, the dagger fell from his grip as his hands came to cup both sides of her face. "Free me from my britches, my queen. No, no—don't use your hands."

Raveena's grin was wicked as she flashed her teeth. Then those teeth went to work undoing the ties that barely held Graham's manhood in check. She buried her nose in his crotch for another deep pull of his scent. Then she got to work undoing the laces, pull by pull.

It was slow work, and Graham did not lift a finger to help her. When she finally got him free, mostly from his eager cock pushing through the fabric, she took her first lick. They both moaned.

Raveena didn't bother with a slow preamble. No, she was too starved for this. She swallowed Graham whole, taking him all the way to the back of her throat in the first go. Her huntsman was a big boy, but he'd let her practice deep-throating him a lot. Enough that she no longer had a gag reflex.

With a fistful of her hair, Graham held her to him. He was no gentleman. He was everything that was rough and rugged. He didn't spend like an untried youth as she swirled her tongue around his tip. He didn't pull away when she used her teeth on the underside of the delicate head of his penis. He wasn't a quick draw as she lapped at his balls. He stood firm and let her lick her fill of him, backing off when he got close and then letting her take him to the back of her throat when he'd caught his breath.

On and on it went like that until he could hold back no longer. He did press her to him then as he let go and spilled into her mouth. Raveena lapped up every drop of him, then licked at the dregs that escaped her mouth and spilled down his still hard cock. When she was done, she sat back on her heels and looked up at her lover with a satisfied grin.

CHAPTER TWELVE

Graham was fucked. Well and truly fucked.

He lay stretched across the width of Raveena's bed, his skin still slick with heat and the aftershocks of her mouth. His eyes were half-closed, his breath slowing. The scent of her clung to his skin—snow lilies and salt and something darker that always rose after she'd had her fill of him.

Raveena was sprawled across his back. Her body was a silken weight, all supple limbs and contented sighs. Her cheek rested against his shoulder blade. Her fingertips moved over the broad plane of his back, tracing idle patterns as if she were trying to write her name on his skin.

The long stem of the R had her nail dragging from the back of his shoulder downward. There was a bite to it, just enough to make his muscles clench. Then the curve of the R, drawn with the soft pad of her finger, looping outward and then back in again across the top of his shoulder blade. A caress with a whisper of possession.

Her fingertip lifted, then pressed down just below to start an A. The angled line bit into his skin with twin strokes—nail again—sharp enough to stir a low growl in his throat. She finished it with a horizontal line across his lower back, this one softer. A soothing stroke after the sting, like balm after a brand.

By the time she curved an E just above his hip, Graham was trembling with want. He wanted to belong to her. He did belong to her.

He'd come into this room to take her crown. With just the tip of her tongue, the tip of her finger, she was rewriting him. Letter by letter. Line by line.

He didn't stop her. He lay still and let her brand him.

Most couples would lie like this in reverse—the woman curled against the man, his body curled around hers, his eyes trained on the door. The protector. The watcher. That was how he and Raveena used to sleep, when everything between them was new and uncertain and touch had to be earned.

Over time, it had changed. This was his favorite— her weight blanketing him, her breath at his neck. It was the only time he ever truly relaxed. Not because he thought she'd defend him from attack. Because when she was on top of him like this, he knew exactly where she was. He had her.

Her fingers paused, then resumed, drawing slow circles over the scar on his shoulder. "Tell me about the war."

He stiffened. His mouth closed, not wanting to offer her any words. That didn't stop the images in his head.

Flashes crowded his mind—fangs and fire. The thunder of troll feet charging across ice, the screams that echoed too long in dark ravines sounding in his ears. He smelled the iron in the snow. Saw the red of the blood. Remembered the names of friends who didn't rise from the frost.

"No," he said, voice low.

"It was that awful." Raveena exhaled, more breath than sigh. "I shouldn't have let you go."

"You couldn't have stopped me."

He felt her shrug. It was the same shrug she gave when an adversary underestimated her.

"Let's talk about my stepdaughter instead. We need to start planning how to deal with her. How to remove her."

"Is that all you really care about?"

"I care about keeping the crown on my head and this castle under my command. I'm a queen. What else is there to care about?"

He shifted beneath her, forcing her to slip from his back. Raveena hit the mattress with a thud and a hiss of surprise. She landed beside him in a tangle of limbs and disheveled hair. The white strands framed her face like fallen snow, but there was nothing soft in her expression—only irritation. Like a cat whose owner rubbed its fur the wrong way.

Graham sat up, chest heaving. The ache in his back from where she'd traced her name still burned like a brand, and gods help him, part of him wanted to drag her back down and mark her the same way. Instead, he answered her rhetorical question.

"You should care about your people. Your lands. Me."

"The people are fed and warm. The land is thriving under my rule. And you—" She reached for him, but he stepped back, standing now, the muscles of his back taut with anger. "You're mine. I have all of it, and I'll keep it, so long as I have the crown and the castle."

Graham laughed—sharp, bitter, a sound torn straight from his chest. He paced away from her, bare feet slapping against the stone floor. The window called to him. Or maybe it was the storm outside, the snow hammering against the glass in thick, relentless sheets.

The cold always came for her. Tried to breach her skin, sink into her bones. The fire always moved away from her, as if even the flames knew better than to get too close to a woman made of frost and fury.

"She can't manage it," Raveena added. "Snow's too naïve. If Charming marries her, we lose everything."

You lose everything, he thought. *Not we. Not the kingdom. You.*

Because all that meant anything to Raveena—was power. And the palace built to reflect it. She didn't know Snow had already moved against her. Didn't know Graham had been the one chosen to end her reign.

He bent and retrieved the dagger from where he'd dropped it. The cool weight of it steadied something in his chest. He wouldn't use it on her, not for a mortal wound. Maybe for a possessive marking. But not tonight.

"Where are you going?" she demanded.

He didn't look at her as he pulled on his trousers. "I have to prepare for the Winter Games."

She cocked her head. "Why?"

He punched his arms into his tunic, yanking it down over his chest. "I've got the urge to gut something."

Raveena reclined lazily on the bed, unabashed in her nakedness, her thighs parting like a promise. "What about my matching pair of bruises?"

Graham turned to look at her. He should have known better. The sight of her always made him putty inside. But he wasn't letting her get her hands on him. Not for a while.

"I'll claim that as my prize. If I win."

"If?" she scoffed. "When you win."

The way she said it—like he couldn't possibly fail, like she believed in him more than anyone ever had—tightened the emotions in his chest. The rage became a smaller ball. The desire flared hotter. And that pissed him off all the more. He growled under his breath because he didn't understand this woman.

In the bed, Raveena clung to him like he was her world. She surrendered everything to him when she was naked. Her body. Her mind. He'd thought that included her heart.

But that organ was cold. Unreachable. No matter what he said. No matter what he did. She would never love him the way that he loved her.

He was just a possession to her. A tool. A piece on the game board.

For him, she was the only thing that ever made him feel whole.

Graham wasn't going to kill her. That had never been in the cards for him. He wasn't going to leave her either. That, her saying her vows to another man, more than any troll, had been the thing that had nearly killed him.

He had two options left. Kill the princess that stood

in the way of his love keeping what she coveted most. Or kill the prince that could give her what she wanted while also standing in Graham's way.

Decisions, decisions.

Blade in hand, fury in his chest, and her scent still on his skin, Graham stormed out the door of the queen's bedroom.

CHAPTER THIRTEEN

The tournament grounds rang with the clash of fists and the roar of a bloodthirsty crowd. The air was bitingly cold—just how Raveena liked it. The icicles were sharp enough to sting the lungs and chase the weak indoors. Snowflakes danced like ash in the air, settling on cloaks, on helms, on the rough-hewn wood of the stands.

The sweat? That was another matter entirely.

Raveena wrinkled her nose as the musk of unwashed bodies wafted past. Men soaked in exertion and testosterone puffed up with pride as they pummeled each other like beasts in rut. Most stank of arrogance, their sweat thick and sour. Graham's was the only scent that didn't offend her sensibilities. The essence that wept from his body held the wild tang of pine and frost, like the wind off the Fenvalen mountains. His sweat she could breathe in like perfume. The rest? Offensive.

Animals brayed and stamped nearby—horses, hounds, even the occasional exotic mount brought in to impress the crowds. Raveena wasn't overly fond of animals. Or the outdoors. Or men who bled on things. The stink of blood and metal and churned earth clung to everything in the arena.

Give her a civilized game played in high-backed chairs, beneath golden chandeliers, where the stakes were thrones and crowns, not bruises and broken teeth. Let others swing swords and grunt in mud; she preferred games with sharper edges—those played with smiles, silence, and secrets. Games where the prize wasn't a battered trophy or fleeting glory but something enduring. Something eternal. Like a kingdom.

She sat atop the carved stone dais beside the other highborn women of the realm. The velvet canopy overhead filtered the morning sun into a cool blue shade. The seats were layered in furs, and goblets of spiced wine were cradled in jeweled hands.

Down below, bare-chested warriors grappled in the ring of packed snow, their bodies slick with exertion, muscles straining under the eyes of queens and princesses who watched with no pretense of modesty. Every time a man landed a blow that sent his opponent to his knees, the ladies tittered behind their gloves, gasped behind their fans.

This wasn't about shock. It was about thrill. The bloodied knuckles, the sharp grunts, the visible power of men pitted against one another—it delighted them.

Raveena leaned back, crossing one leg over the other, her dark gown cascading around her like a pool of ink. Her gaze, cool and curious, scanned the ring— and caught.

Graham stood at the edge of the arena, shirtless, fists taped, the cold wind carving steam from his skin. Snowflakes clung to his hair and shoulders, melting into rivulets that traced the ridges of his muscles. He looked like something out of a dark forest come to steal wandering princesses away. Half-war god, half-wolf— hewn from rage and survival. Dangerous in the way only men who'd seen war and come back sharper could be.

"Is that him?" one lady whispered behind her fan.

"The Wolf of the Troll Wars," said another, breath-less. "I didn't know he was so… large."

Yes, Raveena thought, lips curving faintly as she turned and glared at the two women. *And he's mine*. The girls were smart. They covered their mouths and averted their gazes from both Raveena and Graham.

Good. Let every queen, every daughter, every calcu-lating heiress in the realm watch her man fight. Let them drool and plot and fantasize. But each one had better recognize that Graham Huntsman was off-limits.

He was hers.

Graham stepped into the ring, shoulders rolling, eyes narrowed in concentration. There was a quiet grace to him, even in stillness. His movements foretold of the leashed power of a man who only needed a reason to destroy.

Raveena waited. Waited for the flick of his gaze. For the glance. The acknowledgment that she was there, watching him.

Nothing.

He didn't look at her. Not once. In fact, he prowled to the edge of the ring that was closest to her seat, and then the bastard turned and gave her his back.

Her fingers tightened on the stem of her goblet. So that was how they were going to play it? He was going to ignore her.

Her expression remained cool as she decided her next move. She would let him. Let him try, anyway. Just as she was always eager to sink to her knees when they were alone, he was always eager to find a way to get her alone.

Let him enjoy his little moment in the ring, his crowd of admirers, his noble pretense. Because after this match—win or lose—he'd come to her. And she would remind him of exactly who he belonged to.

A hush fell over the crowd as the announcer stepped into the center of the ring, his voice rising above the wintry din, clear and ceremonial.

"Representing the queen's guard, undefeated in ten tournaments, the pride of Fenvalen, the Wolf of the Troll Wars—Graham Huntsman!"

The crowd erupted. Cheers, stomping boots, raised mugs. Raveena didn't join in. People might know she slept with the wolf. But it would be undignified to make a spectacle of herself in public.

The announcer raised his hand again. "And facing him today—" A pause, the opponent's name came next. Raveena didn't bother to catch it. Something forgettable. A smattering of polite applause followed, but already the crowd's attention had shifted, already their cheers were for the predator, not the prey.

The contender could have been a blacksmith's son, a third-born noble desperate for notice, a drunk with a good punch. It didn't matter. He was about to have his body laid flat in the snow by her wolf.

Graham stepped to the center of the ring like a man doing a chore. No grand gestures. No roaring for the crowd. Just that slow, coiled walk of someone who'd already sized up the fight and found it wanting.

The official gave the nod. The crowd leaned forward. The opponent lunged. It was over in seconds.

One feint. One pivot. One solid punch to the gut

that doubled the fool over, followed by a brutal uppercut that sent him sprawling out of the ring and into the snow.

The audience gasped—then roared. Chairs scraped. Gloves clapped. Ladies squealed behind their hands. Coins changed hands as bets were collected with delighted cheers.

Graham stood over the crumpled body of his opponent. He didn't raise his arms. Didn't nod to the crowd. Didn't look at his queen. Just turned and walked back toward the edge of the ring like he'd taken out the trash.

The ladies' laughter shifted as the murmurs of the court shifted toward the arrival of a late guest. Snow White glided toward the royal box in her usual shade of pale blue. As always, she looked slightly out of place—like she belonged in a nursery rhyme instead of a battlefield gallery. She moved with grace but no fire.

"Running late, dear?" Raveena asked smoothly, her voice laced with frost.

Snow gave a placid smile. "A doe had trouble with her fawn. I couldn't leave her unattended."

Lady Charming leaned forward then, ever the stately viper. "Such care for the helpless. It speaks to your nurturing instincts, Snow. Qualities like that show you'd make an excellent mother."

A murmur of agreement followed. Raveena caught

the not-so-subtle way the older women nodded, measuring wombs as they measured power.

Before Raveena could respond, a ripple moved through the crowd as Prince Charming emerged. The sun struck the polished silver of his armor, drawing cheers from the spectators and delighted sighs from the women in the box. He had that practiced smile on, the one he used when he wanted something.

"Ladies," he said, voice smooth as cream. "Your presence has turned this field of battle into a garden of glory."

A few ladies fluttered like they hadn't heard the same line from his lips a dozen times before.

"For you, my lady..." Charming turned to Snow, taking her gloved hand in his, bending to kiss her knuckles. "I shall win my next bout."

Snow blushed—of course she did—and gave a shy, demure smile.

But then, as Charming's lips pulled away, he turned ever so slightly. And winked. At Raveena.

Raveena had to fight not to roll her eyes right then and there. Because that wink—ridiculous and arrogant and childish as it might be—meant only one thing. She was still in this game of thrones.

She could see it in Charming's smug little smirk: He thought himself clever. Thought he could bed the queen, marry the princess, and hold the loyalty of both.

Let him think he was winning. Let Snow preen like she had been chosen. Let the ladies gossip. The Winter tournament of fists and blood wasn't the only match being played today.

Charming did win his first bout in the games. It wasn't as quick as Graham's. No, the prince drew it out, playing with this opponent. It was all for show. And at the end, he blew a kiss to the princess and gave another lascivious look to the queen.

Yes, he was definitely playing the two of them. Hmm, the kid might be smarter than Raveena gave him credit for. But she saw the board from many angles. And unlike her two naïve opponents, she would adjust her strategy accordingly.

CHAPTER FOURTEEN

It was late in the day, and Graham was already bored and regretting his decision to fight today. Not a single one of his matches had satisfied his bloodlust. How could they when they were over before the second punch?

The sun hung low over the tournament grounds. From his place near the edge of the arena, Graham stood motionless, arms crossed, breath curling in slow, steady puffs. The crowd buzzed behind him—layers of fur and wine and idle chatter—but he heard none of it. His focus narrowed to the man stepping into the ring.

Graham watched the princeling the way a wolf watches prey—still, silent, patient. Charming moved like a show pony in a gilded bridle, tossing smiles to the crowd. His grip on his sword was too relaxed. His stance was all flair and no balance. Footwork too wide. Left side overexposed. Confidence bleeding through the cracks of ignorance.

Prince Charming made fighting look pretty, but it was clear to a trained warrior's eyes that the boy was weak. Graham saw the break in the tree line. The soft underbelly. The moment before the pounce. Charming strutted around the ring, grinning like a cat who thought himself a lion.

The prince made a show of unstrapping his cloak and rolling his shoulders. The crowd cheered, especially the younger nobles. The Ladies' Box stirred with polite interest. Charming soaked in every bit of it, preening, glancing up with a smirk that Graham wanted to wipe clean off his face.

Charming blew a kiss toward Snow, who offered him a demure smile, soft and sweet. The crowd cooed.

That would have been fine. Graham would have ignored the bout like he'd ignored the others. But the fool went and did the one thing Graham could never let slide.

Charming turned ever so slightly—just enough so no one else would notice—and shot a wink toward Raveena.

Graham noticed. He noticed everything about his queen.

He noticed that her posture was impeccable, as

always. But he caught the tension in her shoulders, the slight shift in her weight. The cushion beneath her must've been worn thin because she kept favoring her right side, adjusting every few minutes like the seat had betrayed her spine.

He noticed her wine goblet resting untouched on the arm of her throne. She'd sipped once, early on, then wrinkled her nose so slightly it might've been mistaken for a twitch. Clearly, the vintage wasn't to her liking.

And that girl chattering behind Raveena's shoulder? Every time the woman spoke, a flicker of irritation passed over Raveena's face, a micro-expression that anyone else might've missed. Anyone except him. Raveena never tolerated simpering. If the girl was still sitting there, it was only because Raveena needed something from her. Some piece of gossip, a promise, a pawn.

He noticed that she caught the princeling's wink. She gave no outward sign that she noticed. But Graham knew, and it made his fists clench.

Not because the wink was bold. Not because it was shameless. Because he knew exactly what that wink meant.

The prince thought that she was still his.

Like hell she was.

Graham turned, jaw grinding, and called out to the other soldiers gathered around him.

"Let the prince win."

They blinked at him. One soldier's brows drew together, eyes darting to the ring as if he'd misheard. Another grimaced, his hand tightening on the hilt of his blade like it itched to be used instead. A third exchanged a glance with his companion, a frown carved deep between his eyes. Confusion rippled through the group like a stone dropped in still water.

"Let him win?" Corwin spoke each word carefully, as though said again would reveal the true meaning. "You've seen him fight. He hits like a snowflake."

Another man snorted. "We could all take him down with one hand tied and the other holding a drink."

"But you're going to lose anyway," Graham said.

A pause. Glares. Then, in unison—"Why?"

"Because I want him. He's mine."

That earned some raised brows and a few chuckles.

"Can I at least make him bleed?" Corwin asked.

Graham shrugged.

"Fine." Corwin rubbed the back of his neck. "But you're buying every damn round tonight."

"Top shelf," Graham agreed.

That got them moving. Over the next hour, one by one, the soldiers entered the ring. One by one, they fell. Not believably, not really—staggering after light blows, crumpling like sacks of flour. The crowd, drunk and eager for drama, didn't question it. They cheered, laughed, called out encouragements.

The prince played his part perfectly. He grinned broader with each "victory," arms raised like a boy playing at hero.

When the match was called, the soldiers rose from the snow and stumbled out of the arena, still playing their parts. Until they got to Graham. That's when they shot Graham sharp glares—equal parts begrudging respect and irritation. He'd owe them more than their weight in drinks after this.

Graham didn't care. Because in one heartbeat, everything shifted. His gaze lifted—he hadn't meant to, had been avoiding it all day—but it found her.

Raveena reclined in her seat like a goddess carved from ebony and ivory, dark gown curling around her legs like mist. Her lips were red, her eyes unreadable, and when their eyes met across the snow-packed arena, the world narrowed.

She saw him. She saw everything.

The crooked choreography. The sudden rise of the prince. The deliberate shaping of the bracket so that Graham would meet Charming one on one.

She was a master at games, and she knew. Instead of fury, instead of disdain, she smiled. Her eyes gleamed with amusement. Her brow arched with approval.

She didn't care about Charming. Never had. Not the

man, not his pride, not the game he thought he was playing. She wanted Graham to take him down.

And gods, that did something to him.

More than the wins. More than the coming fight. That—that look. That partnership between them.

It hit Graham low and hard, curling around his ribs and blooming in his chest like a crack in the ice across a pond. Because this—this was what he wanted. Not just her body, not just her pleasure, not even her crown.

He wanted her alongside him. Matching his stride. Plotting with him. Fighting beside him.

They were dangerous alone. But together? They could rule the world.

He stepped toward the ring, eyes on the prize. It was no longer about revenge or pride. It was about her.

The crowd pulsed around the ring, a tide of anticipation and frostbitten breath rising in a roar as Graham stepped into the ring. The packed snow thinned by the blood and sweat of matches already won. The cold barely registered against his skin. The sting in his knuckles had long since faded. He'd climbed the bracket like a storm tearing through shutters. No opponent had lasted more than a few heartbeats.

Now the crowd wanted a finale. Now they wanted a show. And Graham? He hadn't decided whether they'd get one.

Across from him, Prince Charming paced with a

smirk painted across his face. His golden hair too polished. His armor unnecessarily gleaming. He moved like a man who'd never taken a hit that mattered.

"They call you the wolf," Charming said, tossing a lazy shoulder roll, his voice just loud enough for only Graham to catch.

Graham didn't respond. He simply stared.

Charming chuckled, cocky as ever. "The wolf who hides under the queen's bed. She has a nice thread count, doesn't she? The antlers of her headboard are an excellent grip for a man to brace himself as he takes her."

Ah. So the fight would be quick.

The whistle blew. Charming surged forward with all the grace of a dancing rooster. His first punch came fast but not sharp. Graham sidestepped without effort, his eyes never leaving the prince's.

Charming blinked. Then tried again.

This time, Graham let the punch land. The prince's fist caught him on the cheek. His head barely turned. The crowd gasped. Corwin was right. The boy hit like a snowflake.

Graham's eyes narrowed, cold and amused.

Charming gulped.

What followed wasn't a match. It was a lesson. Blow after blow came—each one weaker than the last, each one a study in desperation. Graham moved through them like smoke through fingers. Sometimes he let them land just to prove how little they mattered. He didn't even lift his hands. Because this boy—this spoiled, soft-palmed peacock—was nothing.

This was the man Raveena might marry? This was who the court thought worthy of ruling beside her? She'd eat him alive.

And that was the point.

That's why she wanted him. Because he was easy. Like the old king. Like every man before Graham who had mistaken the gift of Raveena's body for her power and her crown for her, a love she would never give them.

They were never strong enough to hold her. But Graham? He didn't want to hold her. He wanted to stand beside her. And that meant playing the long game.

Charming swung again, sloppy and winded. But it connected.

Graham took one slow breath. Then he sank—first to one knee, then the other. The cold bit through his trousers. He placed one hand to the ground, curled his fingers into the ice-packed dirt, and tapped once.

The crowd froze. The roar died. Even the wind seemed to pause.

The official stepped forward, stunned. "The Wolf... taps out? Victory to Prince Charming."

Silence.

Charming raised his arms, confused but grinning, looking around like maybe he'd earned something.

The crowd was slow to cheer. But they did. How could they not with those golden good looks that should clearly best a dark beast like Graham on his knees?

Graham's eyes found her. Raveena was still seated in the Ladies' Box, lips parted in surprise. Then they pursed in mounting anger. She was pissed. His queen wasn't used to being outmaneuvered.

CHAPTER FIFTEEN

The village reeked of wood smoke, sweat, and ale. Mud slicked the narrow stone paths between the soldiers' quarters, half-frozen in the chill dusk air. The clamor of laughter, tankards clanking, and celebratory boasts echoed around her. Raveena moved through it all like a blade slicing silk.

Men caught sight of her and looked away. Some bowed low, others stiffened with the reflex of discipline. None met her gaze. None dared speak.

She wore no crown tonight. No ceremonial robes. Only a deep plum cloak lined in sable and a simple gown that clung to her hips and moved like shadow. Still, she was unmistakably a queen. The queen.

Queen Raveena didn't spare the men a glance.

She found Corwin tucked into the crook of a stone

archway, lips deep in a kiss with a wide-eyed noble girl who looked young enough to still believe in ballads. The girl gasped at Raveena's approach. She scrambled to smooth her skirts and disappeared into the background like a frightened rabbit.

"Where is he?"

Corwin cleared his throat. He reached for his tankard with one hand and jerked his thumb with the other toward the far end of the hall. "Last door on the right."

Raveena didn't thank him. She strode to the closed wooden door. Without bothering to knock, she pushed it open.

Graham stood inside, shirtless, the fire low in the hearth behind him. He was angled toward a small mirror, dabbing at the dark bloom spreading across his jawline. Her fingers twitched at her sides at the sight of the bruise.

He didn't look surprised to see her. Just glanced up. Then went back to examining the damage like she wasn't even there.

Raveena crossed the room in two strides. She snatched the cloth from his hand, tossed it away, and pressed her fingers to his jaw.

Graham caught her wrist before she could apply the healing spell. "I'll keep my bruises, thank you."

"Fool," she hissed.

He didn't deny it. "I gave you what you wanted. Your prince bested your beast. That should make him worthy of you."

Raveena curled her fingers into the palms of her hands.

"That is what you wanted, isn't it, Your Majesty?"

Graham's bruise was starting to darken. Rich violet spread like spilled ink beneath his skin. She grabbed another cloth from a side table, dipped it in the bowl of water, and pressed it gently to the swelling, dabbing instead of healing.

He let her. But his words didn't stop.

"Or is that if he marries Snow, the whole realm will see the truth? That the prince and princess are weak. While the true queen and the wolf stand cast aside… yet still stronger than either of them. Is that what you want, Ray?"

Her gaze caught his. Ice blue met coal black. And there it was again—that mind she loved. That brutal logic. That ability to think two, three, four moves ahead. Raveena had thought she played the game best. But Graham had seen the board more clearly; her wolf had lost the fight to win the war.

"I'll have my reward now," he said, voice low, eyes locked to hers.

Not a question. Not a request. A claim. And gods, she wanted to be claimed.

"You didn't win," she said.

"Didn't I?"

Graham's eyes burned into hers—dark, sure, unrelenting. For a breathless second, Raveena wondered if he would speak again. Demand more, demand everything.

Instead, he kissed her.

It wasn't soft. It wasn't sweet. It wasn't even a claiming. Because she was already his. No, this kiss was an assertion. A period at the end of a declarative statement.

Graham's mouth crushed against hers with a hunger so fierce it felt like flame erupting through her chest. Raveena gasped into it, then melted. She pressed back, matching his fire with ice of her own. She tangled her fingers in his hair, dragged him closer, opened her mouth, and devoured him like she had been dying of thirst for the last three years.

Because she had.

Every night without him had been airless, dry, aching. Every kiss before him had tasted like ash. But this—This was everything.

She pulled him deeper, angling her mouth to take more, to taste him fully, as if she could swallow his breath and fuse him back into her skin. Graham let her ravage him—let her be greedy, wild, reckless—and then he gave it right back. Teeth, tongue, lips—his kiss was savage and merciless and utterly him.

He gripped her waist, turned, and shoved her back. The mattress caught her.

She bounced. Her hair fanned around her face. Her lips parted from the kiss that hadn't ended so much as detonated.

Raveena gasped—and then smiled. That slow, dangerous smile she only gave him. Because Graham knew. He knew how to touch her, how to push her. How to take all the cold iron she wore like armor and heat it.

She'd trusted no one—not with her body, not with her crown, not with her soul.

Except him.

Because he knew what she needed.

To hurt. Just a little.

Not to be punished. But to feel. For a woman born of winter and crowned in frost, pain was the only thing sharp enough to pierce the numbness.

Her legs fell open in invitation, gown tangled at her thighs. She met his gaze with fire licking at the edges of her smile.

"Take me," she said, voice rough with breath and need.

"You're nowhere near wet enough for me. Fix that. Now."

She knew what he wanted. She reached under her dress and hooked her thumbs in the band of her panties. She didn't give him a show, didn't pull them down slow and seductively. Raveena was too impatient to get her prize.

She ripped the panties off. Discarded the fabric onto the floor. Then she touched herself.

Around and around her index and middle finger went. Circling her clit. Tugging at her labials. Dipping into the center of her sex.

She didn't need finesse to make herself come. She just needed his gaze on her. The command in his eyes was enough to push her over the edge. Raveena came in under five minutes.

"Good girl. Do it again."

She whimpered, but she didn't argue. She knew her Graham. He would not be moved until he was satisfied. And he was a big boy. It was a fair point that she needed to be good and wet when he took her.

"If you add your tongue, I'll be ready faster."

"Did I ask for your opinion, Ray? Get those lazy fingers back to work. If I take you now, I'll hurt you."

"I want it to hurt a little."

Graham cupped the big tent in his pants. "It'll hurt a lot."

She grinned, throwing her head back as she pumped her fingers in and out of herself as rough as she could make it. It wasn't rough enough. "I've been using my fingers for three years, pretending they were yours. But they're not thick enough. Not blunt enough. There are no calluses. Just the thought of you crooking your index finger is enough to get me off. I'd be sitting on my throne, with my court assembled around me, and I'd imagine I'd see you in the shadows of the halls, beckoning me with that finger, and I'd have to press my thighs to—ah!"

The rough hands she had been dreaming about grabbed her thighs. Graham turned her over. Her front bounced once on the mattress. The palm of his hand came to her back and pressed her roughly into the bedding. Her dress was rucked up, her ass exposed to him.

Raveena heard the rustle of fabric. She felt the heat of his thick cock against her ass cheeks. If he took her in her rear entrance without any preparation, that would surely hurt. But she'd take it. She'd take him any way she could get him.

Graham didn't press his cock into her ass. He spread her core apart, aimed for her entrance, and struck true.

They both cried out as he bottomed out inside her. He'd been right. She wasn't wet enough for him. The burn was so good Raveena pressed her fists into the mattress to raise her ass higher, to press herself back and get more of him into her. He could never be deep enough. She had him where she wanted him, where he belonged, buried inside her so deep that she couldn't tell where he ended and she began.

His hand went around her throat. Those calluses pressed into her neck, constricting her air supply.

"Tell me you're mine," he growled.

"Yours," she gasped. "Always." She tried to inhale but barely got a whisper of air. Still, she managed. "Forever."

Graham roared in her ear as they both came. Raveena's intimate muscles clamped down on him as he poured his seed into her womb. When she returned to her rooms later, she would take no tinctures to avoid the possibility of what might come from their coupling. Before she passed out from the pleasure and the lack of oxygen, she prayed to the God Mothers that his seed would take root.

CHAPTER SIXTEEN

He was still hard.

Graham had taken Raveena from behind, holding her down while thrusting deep until the slap of his balls on her clit made her come a third time. Before she'd come to, he'd rolled her to her side, shoving her knees into her chest and tugging handfuls of her hair until her head bent back and her hips curved helplessly into his as he dove deeper into her core with his cock. She regained consciousness as her muscles squeezed his in another orgasm. Then he flattened her on her back, holding her hands over her head, tossing her legs over his shoulders and piling into her still slick cunt until she begged for mercy.

He showed her none. Because he knew the mercy she asked for was not for him to stop. She needed the claiming as much as he needed to stake ownership over every part of her in every manner that she could be taken.

Hours later, he was still hard. Exhausted but raring for another go. That's how it always was with her. Graham would never get enough of this woman. And she would never deny him.

Even when she'd married the king, she hadn't considered barring Graham from her bed. The problem lay with him because he couldn't stomach sharing her with another.

"I'm going to have to kill the princeling."

Raveena lifted a brow at him even as her eyes remained closed. "After our wedding night, when I seal ownership of the crown, you can do what you like with Charming."

"You're not marrying that twat."

"Fine." She lifted one bare shoulder in a shrug. "Then you'll kill Snow for me."

"There's been enough killing, Ray."

"There'll be more deaths if I lose my crown."

Graham hunched down in the bed until he was nose to nose with her. Languidly, she opened her eyes. The blue ice made him burn.

"I won't let anyone take the crown or the castle from you. Every man from Fenvalen and Everfrost will fall in line behind me after I've brought them home from the war. You have your tenterhooks in me. Where you go, I'll follow. So you'll have an army behind you."

She gazed at him, her expression unreadable. "I've always been confused about that expression. Is it tender hooks? Or tenterhooks?"

"Does it matter? If anyone comes for your crown, they have to go through me first. And no one is getting past me to get to you. It would be war."

Raveena huffed and rolled her eyes. "I didn't orchestrate a peace to put you back into war, Graham."

"I won that war."

"Of course you did." She waved dismissively. "My plan now is far more elegant and less bloody. Kill either Snow or Charming, and my path is clear. Or kill them both. Then there's no need for armies to fight."

"Do you think I can't best Charming's pretty boy army?"

"It's not Charming I'm worried about. These are queens that we'd be fighting, not mindless trolls."

The fire in the corner had burned down to a whisper, casting long shadows along the rough-hewn stone walls. Graham lay on his back, one arm flung over his eyes, his chest rising and falling in the slow, heavy rhythm of a man undone. Beside him, Raveena sprawled in the curve of his body, all soft limbs and sharp silence. Her skin was still damp with sweat, her pale hair tangled across his chest like a banner.

He wanted to roll over on his stomach and hitch her onto his back. But he didn't feel the need. He knew she wasn't going anywhere. She was his—physically, at least. If there was a way he could reach into her heart and pull that organ to him, he would. But as always, it was her head that he was fighting with. More aptly, the phantom crown on her head that she would give up for no one.

They'd moved like a storm and fire when their bodies were joined, all fury and possession. Now the quiet settled in. And with it, the ache behind Graham's eyes sharpened. His focus shifted to the real problem between them.

Charming.

He gritted his teeth, jaw twitching. The prince's smug wink. His cheap jabs. That ridiculous victory.

"Are you still brooding over the match?"

"You let him touch you." Why hadn't he at least broken one of the boy's fingers when he'd had the chance?

"It was once," she said. "And it was not memorable."

"I hate that his bony ass stank up your sheets."

"I didn't take him to *my* bed. I've never had anyone in my bed but you."

Graham wanted to believe her. Gods, he almost did. But a small, cruel part of him whispered *liar*, and he didn't silence it. He just didn't say it aloud.

Raveena had had her husband for three years. Likely other lovers. She'd had them before Graham. It wasn't frowned upon for future queens to kick up their skirts for a bit of fun. Not before their unions, not during their reigns. Graham was certain that when he and Raveena were together, there had been no one else. That same certainty escaped him now.

Graham turned away from her. He stared at the ceiling, watching the shadows shift. He was tired. Not in body. His body had found its relief, its center. But his mind was fraying.

He was sick of secrets. Sick of plots and masks. Sick of silent wars waged in ballrooms with fake smiles.

He was a soldier. And he wanted clarity.

"I'm not going to kill her."

Raveena blinked her eyes open. Her gaze was slow to focus.

"Snow. I'm not going to spill her blood. I know you want her gone. I know she's a threat. But murder…" Graham exhaled. "I'll take her. Kidnap her. Smuggle her into one of the border realms. Somewhere in some faraway woods. She likes nature. She might even be happier."

Raveena said nothing. She propped herself up on one elbow, eyes dark.

"If she's gone, the crown stays on your head. There's no need for you to marry that simpering fool. No need to risk the people turning on you if she claims her birthright."

Raveena's lips parted—whether to argue, to thank him, or to scheme, Graham couldn't tell. Before she could speak, a knock shattered the hush.

A low, irritated growl rumbled from Graham's throat. "I'm busy," he barked.

Corwin's voice answered, muffled through the wood. "I'm not here for you, Wolf. I'm here for the queen. She's needed."

Raveena sat up, the sheets sliding from her bare shoulders. "What is it?"

"We've received word from the castle."

A pause.

"Snow White went missing."

CHAPTER SEVENTEEN

There was still the musk of sex on Raveena as she entered the chamber. She hadn't had time to go back to her rooms and change. She didn't plan to be away from her lover too long. Why bathe off what she fully intended to put back on her skin, in her mouth, in every orifice of her body?

The moment after she finished playing the part of patient stepmother to her stepdaughter's tantrum, Raveena would be returning to her lover to pick up where they left off. This time, she would demand that Graham claim her in the remaining orifice he hadn't touched since his return.

He'd been the only man to ever enter her backdoor. Hell, he was the only man she ever let take her from behind. Her wolf was the only person she trusted to be that close to her while she couldn't see him. Just thinking about it made her ache to be filled by him. She needed to get this over with quickly.

Raveena's hand drifted to her throat as she walked, fingers brushing over the faint ache blooming just beneath her jaw. She winced. A bruise. The ghost of Graham's grip from when he'd pulled her to him— mouths clashing, breath shared, a kiss less about affection and more about possession. She'd grown used to concealing such marks. Her magic responded before she even called on it, pooling at her fingertips, ready to smooth over the evidence like always.

But as she passed a mirror in the corridor, something made her pause.

The bruise wasn't just a smear of shadow beneath her pale skin. It curved, perfectly placed, a dusky band that sat at the base of her throat like a necklace—no, a collar. She stared at it, pulse stuttering. It was almost elegant in its placement, like a deliberate brand. Not from a careless lover but a master who marked what was his.

A shiver rippled down her spine. She was his. Entirely. Willingly.

The magic curled back into her fingers, unspent. She let her hands fall to her sides. Pulling the cloak tighter around her shoulders, she decided to hide the secret adornment from the world.

She knew she should wipe the smile from her face before facing her audience. Queens were ruthless. But she was too full, too sated to concern herself.

The chamber was a contradiction—opulent and ruthless, much like the women who ruled within it. Velvet drapes the color of crushed berries hung heavy over the frost-rimmed windows, muffling the sounds of the howling wind outside. A crystal chandelier glittered above, each shard humming faintly with captured magic, casting prismatic light over the war-scarred stone walls. The long Frostfire Table dominated the room, carved from a single slab of glacial obsidian veined with flickers of silver that pulsed faintly with heat. It was said to have been forged in the heart of a fallen star—beautiful, unyielding, and cold.

Around it sat the queens, princesses, and strategists of the realm, their bodies draped in silk and fur, their minds honed like blades. Behind them, maps lined the walls, dotted with glowing sigils and animated tokens that moved across borders in real time. A rack of scrolls stood in one corner, flanked by a rack of spears. Beneath their jeweled slippers, the floor was polished stone, scored with faint gouges from past battles and boots—scars of decisions made and challenged in this very room.

They turned toward her as one, seated in a crescent arc around the Frostfire Table, their expressions carved from varying degrees of worry, suspicion, and quiet hunger.

"Snow White is missing," said Lady Tern, her white-gold braid looped over one shoulder like a serpent.

"Are you certain my stepdaughter is not out in the woods looking after a dove with a broken wing or a mouse caught in a trap?"

"The stables were in disarray. Broken reins. A bloodied saddlecloth. We suspect foul play."

Raveena stopped just shy of the circle. Her face was composed. Inside her mind was a storm. Someone had taken Snow? Someone had done her dirty work for her? But who?

"Where were you, Queen Raveena, when the precious girl went missing?" Lady Charming turned from the fire, gaze full of accusation.

Raveena didn't flinch. She lifted her chin higher. The soft shift of her shoulders caused her cloak to part at the collar, revealing the unmistakable bruises at her neck. Dark and tender, shaped by desire, Graham's marks bloomed like violets against snow-pale skin.

Her lips curved in a slow, measured smile—one that balanced disdain and amusement with effortless precision. "I was otherwise engaged."

A few of the ladies arched painted brows. One or two exchanged looks. And then—there it was—the smallest twitch of a smile on Lady Hollowmere's mouth. The smirk in Queen Elsbeth's eyes. The entire barracks had seen her enter the soldiers' quarters. And by the sounds that likely echoed through the stone walls… heard what happened next.

Raveena didn't need to name Graham. The knowing looks said enough. She had, indeed, been otherwise engaged. Certainly not hiding in the stables with a blade in her hand.

Still, the timing was too perfect. Her carefully laid plans interrupted. Her pawn removed from the board before she could make the move herself.

Raveena's hands were clean. But her thoughts were anything but. Who had done this before she could?

The door slammed open. Prince Charming stormed in, his hair windblown, eyes wild. His armor appeared buckled hastily, as if he hadn't fully dressed before galloping to the castle. "What are you all doing? Sitting here sipping wine while the princess is missing?"

Lady Veyne narrowed her eyes. "You dare barge into this chamber and address queens in this manner?"

"You forget yourself, princeling," said Queen Elsbeth, her voice low and lethal.

"I will be king of Thornhall once I wed."

"If you wed," Lady Charming interjected, rising now, her hand firm on her son's shoulder. "We must find Snow White first or there will be no ceremony."

Charming stepped forward, brushing his mother's

hand away. "I will search every cavern and cursed path from here to the edge of the realm to bring her back," he declared. "So that she may stand beside me when I marry—"

He turned, eyes locking with Raveena's.

"—Queen Raveena."

CHAPTER EIGHTEEN

The stable doors had been thrown open. Fresh snow blew in, crusting along the threshold. Broken reins hung like snapped tendons from the stalls. A saddle lay discarded in the aisle, one stirrup torn, the other twisted as though yanked in haste or desperation.

Graham stood just inside the entrance. Behind him, his soldiers fanned out. The torches on the stable walls guttered in the cold wind. The horses, still in their stalls, shifted restlessly, nickering low, their breath ghosting in the frigid air. They smelled the tension.

So did he.

At first glance, it looked like an ambush. Boot prints scuffed into the dirt. Blood on the wood near the back exit. The tang of magic still lingering in the air, faint but sharp—like the final crackle before a fire goes cold.

"Looks like she was dragged out," Corwin muttered, crouched near the trampled straw. "See this line here? Body weight."

"Mm," Graham answered, but he wasn't convinced.

He stepped farther in, scanning the chaos, not for what was obvious but what was missing. Too much mess. Too perfectly imperfect.

The blood, for one—barely a few drops, and only in one place, as if someone had placed it there. Then there were the broken reins. It was a clean break. They weren't frayed. They'd been cut.

And there—he knelt—hoofprints. Clear. Unhurried. Leading out of the stables and into the woods. A calm departure. Not a scramble.

"Look at this." The others moved closer as Graham touched his fingers to the indentations. "Whoever took the horse didn't flee. There's no struggle here. The animal wasn't panicked. No gallop. No chaos."

Corwin frowned. "You saying it was staged?"

"I'm saying that whatever this was, it wasn't a kidnapping." Graham rose to his full height. "She went willingly."

"Then who staged the mess?" Corwin asked. "Who leaves false blood, snapped tack, to make it look like she was taken?"

Graham's mind was already turning, gears grinding behind his tight jaw. Snow was no fool. Naïve, maybe. Soft around the edges, certainly. But behind those dove-gray eyes was a calculating little monarch-in-the-making. She'd planned to murder a queen.

She had vanished, that much was clear. It wasn't without a trace. She wanted them to think she hadn't planned it. But the question was—

Who did she leave with? Who had the stealth? The knowledge of this place? The access?

There were too many variables. Too many hands in the dark. And worse—too many of them not his.

"Clean this up," he said to Corwin, his voice like gravel. "Get the guards back on patrol. Make it look like we're searching with the rest of them."

"You're not staying?" Corwin asked.

Graham shook his head once. "I need to find out who Snow trusted enough to run away with," he said. "And what the hell she plans to do next."

Because this wasn't just a girl disappearing. It was the board shifting. What if he was chasing the wrong enemy?

As the men scattered into the night, lanterns bobbing in the darkness, Graham pulled his cloak tighter around his shoulders and started the climb back toward the castle. The cold bit at his face. Raveena might be a queen made of strategy and secrets, but even a queen couldn't play the right hand if she didn't know all the cards.

He needed her to know everything. He needed her to see Snow clearly. Not as a naïve girl grasping at a crown. As a woman capable of playing dirty.

He thought of Raveena's face when she planned, when her mind clicked into that deadly rhythm. He wanted to be beside her when that happened. Wanted to plan with her. Win with her.

Not just be her sword. But her match. Her equal. Her partner.

Graham prowled through the stone halls, boots muffled by runner rugs, hand resting lightly on the hilt of his dagger as he navigated the familiar passages by memory. Torchlight flickered low along the corridor walls, casting long, licking shadows that danced over his shoulders. The scent of wax and old stone filled his lungs as he made his way to her rooms.

The guards had changed shifts. Servants had retired. He hoped the queen had returned to her chambers and not his. Though the idea of her in his bed made his dick hard. Harder.

He didn't knock. He slipped through the door of her chambers like he had so many times before—sometimes invited, sometimes not.

The room was neat, symmetrical to the point of obsession. Chessboards arranged with half-played games. Puzzles waiting for final pieces. A carved wooden box on the table, slightly ajar, filled with perfectly sharpened quills. This was Raveena distilled: ordered, strategic, always thinking three moves ahead.

It was the bed that caught his eye. Graham moved toward it slowly, warily. The sheets were smooth, tucked with precision. The scent of her skin lingered in the linens from last night—jasmine oil and sweat and sin. His sin. Their sin.

And yet…

He remembered how Charming had smirked during their fight, had spat those words like a man certain of his conquest. What was it the boy had said about her thread count? And her headboard? Her sheets were silk —no thread count to boast. The headboard was a latticework of dark metal.

What had the boy prince been going on about? Charming hadn't lied. Raveena had confirmed they'd slept together. Graham had seen the child's bruises on her inner thigh.

A sound pulled Graham's attention toward the adjoining chamber—the old king's room. The door stood slightly ajar. A sliver of pale moonlight cut through the gap.

Graham moved to it. He pushed the door open. And stopped dead in his tracks.

There, at the center of the room, stood the king's

bed. The piece of furniture was an opulent monstrosity of masculine vanity. The headboard was forged from deer antlers, their gnarled tines splayed like a crown of bone, polished smooth but still cruel in their curve. The sheets looked obscenely soft, like they'd been made to cradle a newborn babe. The fabric was the kind that whispered wealth with every shift and wrinkle. Cotton so fine and tightly woven it had to be counted in the thousands.

It hit Graham like a punch to the gut. Raveena had told the truth. She'd never had Charming—or even her late husband—in her bed.

The one place she let herself rest each night. The one place she let down her guard. She had only ever welcomed him in there.

"I expected a servant. But I suppose the queen's dog escapes his leash every now and again."

Prince Charming stepped out from the side chamber, drying his hands on a monogrammed cloth that was wrapped around his waist. He rested his fists on his hips, feet akimbo, like he owned the damn place. The boy wore a smirk, half-lidded and lazy. His hair was tousled artfully, as if he'd just finished another preening in the mirror.

Graham's hand dropped to his dagger, excited for the chance to carve more than one bruise into that pretty face.

CHAPTER NINETEEN

"Your Majesty, perhaps now is the time to revisit the treaty we discussed—"

"My daughter is of age and would make a fine addition to your council—"

"I've already begun embroidering a swaddling blanket—just in case…"

Raveena kept walking. Her spine was straight, her mouth neutral, her eyes the glinting gray of a glacier. She made no promises. No denials. She simply nodded or offered a low hum of acknowledgment and let the crush of silk and whispers part before her like mist.

Inside, however, her thoughts spun. The moment Charming had made his proclamation, the women had turned like vines to sunlight. Desperate to graft themselves to what they assumed would be the next axis of power.

It was predictable. It was tedious. It was… disappointing.

There was no sport in their moves. No strategy. Just desperation and court polish.

Snow's disappearance had brought a flicker of challenge. That move hadn't been in Raveena's game book. It hadn't even felt like one of the court's ploys. Which meant it was something else entirely.

Raveena wanted to puzzle it out. Not Charming. Definitely not with these simpering diplomats following hot on her trail. She wanted Graham.

Graham, with his sharp mind, his grounded instincts. She wanted to feel his voice low in her ear while he pointed out clues others missed. Wanted his hands wrapped around her waist as they conspired over theories in the quiet of her chambers.

She was almost there. She was nearly free from the melee, just feet from the tall frostwood doors, when Lady Charming swept into her path like a silken scythe.

"My dear," Lady Charming said, smiling so tightly her teeth clicked. "You must be overwhelmed. Such attention, and now my son's beautiful declaration."

Raveena tilted her head, expression still placid. "Declaration?"

Lady Charming's smile grew pinched. "He's chosen

wisely. You'll bring strength to the line. Of course, you'll accept his proposal."

Raveena let one brow arch. "Will I?"

Lady Charming blinked. "Of course. It's the only path that lets you keep that crown on your head."

"Is it?" Raveena asked, her voice velvet-wrapped steel.

The older woman's mouth parted. Raveena moved past her before the retort could find breath. She didn't get far.

A girl stood at the edge of the hallway—a young woman, perhaps just past her debut. Her gown was modest but expertly tailored. Her bearing was straight-backed, as though she had been raised in the presence of royalty. She didn't curtsy. She didn't smile.

Raveena was certain she'd never seen her in the Frost Court. But something about the girl held her attention. The stillness of her. The weight behind her gaze. A queen-in-waiting, no doubt.

The girl stepped forward and dipped her head. "Queen Raveena. I'm Princess Aurora."

Yes, she knew this girl. Aurora was the betrothed of Prince Phillip of the Forest Kingdom. Or at least she had been. Raveena's spies in the Coastal Kingdom had sent her a missive that the sea, forest, and coast kingdoms were playing a rousing game of musical thrones. When the music stopped, no one was with the bride or groom that had been prescribed to them. And now one of the players was here in her court.

"I believe I may know where Snow White has gotten off to."

"And how would you know that?"

Princess Aurora lifted a delicate hand, her fingers closing over the silver clasp of her cloak. "She sent me a letter. I have it in my carriage."

Raveena studied her. The girl didn't flinch. There was steel there. Ambition, to be sure.

Interesting.

Raveena gave a small nod. "Lead the way, Princess."

She followed the girl out of the great hall, leaving the other women behind. The frost-touched doors closed behind them like the lid of a box snapping shut. Raveena exhaled.

"You made it here to the Frost Kingdom quickly with Snow's disappearance."

"We were passing through."

"We?"

Princess Aurora nodded but didn't elaborate. "I had started a correspondence with Snow some years ago. I thought I'd stop in and visit."

"How lovely."

The night was bitter. Shards of ice glittered on the stone walkways. Frost crept in, branching patterns along the carriages lined up outside the Winter Court's northern hall. The scent of firewood and something fishy —seaweed, perhaps—clung faintly to the young princess, wafting back each time her cloak fluttered in the breeze.

Aurora turned, her face soft in the moonlight. "It's just inside. I didn't want to risk carrying it in, in case it was intercepted. I thought you would understand."

Raveena did understand. Far too well. She did not climb into the carriage as instructed. "I've played this game too long to walk into a trap without knowing whose move it is."

Aurora's polite smile didn't waver. But her eyes darkened ever so slightly. "You think I would trick you?"

"I think you're not the innocent girl you pretend to be."

"You're right about that. I lost my innocence years ago. As do most princesses slated to live a life not of her choosing."

"What is it that you want, Aurora?"

"What every girl wants. To love whom she chooses freely."

Funny. That was what Raveena wanted, too. That and her castle. She wanted Graham and her castle. This little girl was singing Raveena's tune.

No. That was someone else singing. The song was

so sweet. So achingly beautiful, it bent Raveena to her knees.

The door to the carriage opened. A girl sat inside. Her red curls were wild in the wind. Her lips parted in a melody that shimmered through the air like spun sugar and silk. The notes wrapped around Raveena's thoughts like warm hands. She knew—knew—somewhere deep inside that she should cover her ears, turn away, run.

The music poured through her veins like honeyed wine. Her eyelids grew heavy. Her body swayed. And then she felt nothing but calm and sleepy as she stepped willingly into the carriage.

CHAPTER TWENTY

"I was brought here to court the Snow Princess, but I've decided to have the Snow Queen instead."

The king's chambers reeked of clove oil and mothballs. The grandeur of it was lacquered over with age. Heavy drapes sagged at the windows, their velvet faded, their tassels dulled with time. The rugs were thick but fraying at the edges. The furniture was grand but stiff, as if no one had sat in it for a decade without armor or gout. Dust floated like lazy ghosts in the shafts of moonlight, cutting through the tall arched panes, and the fire in the hearth sputtered like it too was on its last legs.

And yet, there stood the golden boy prince. Towel slung low on his hips. His tunic lay crumpled on the floor beside a discarded sash, one boot tipped on its side near the hearth, the other nowhere in sight. A silver comb had been left askew on the vanity. A wine goblet—half-full, staining the edge in a careless ring—perched precariously on an ancient table carved for kings, not playboys.

That pissed Graham off more than the boy's words. Raveena loathed disorder. She kept her life, her castle, her image, in perfect lines and polished corners. The sight of Charming's chaos, his carelessness, was just galling. Graham wanted to slice off the prince's bare feet that had tracked water through the room. His fingers itched to reach for his blade, to run the golden boy through right there. But his eyes flicked to the snow bear's pelt beneath the prince's bare feet. One drop of blood would ruin the rug. Raveena would be more furious about the bloodstain than the corpse.

"Mother wanted me to court the girl. And I did. But gods, she bored me. Always pouting or preening or pretending to be above it all. Raveena, though—she's a woman. Sharp. Hungry. She doesn't wait to be caught; she hunts. She chased after me, while I always had to chase Snow. That gets tiring, you know. Wears on a man's ego."

Graham's hands curled into fists. Not because of the insult. Because part of him knew that Charming believed every word. And Raveena—his Raveena—had let him believe it.

"Don't worry, wolf. I won't bar you from the queen's bed once we wed." Charming waved a bejeweled hand at the king's bed, then sat his bare ass down on the sheets as he toweled himself dry. "I prefer maids to these royal ladies. Common women will bop on top of you all night long. A noblewoman will expect a chap to do all the thrusting until they reach a climax. I don't have to tell you how hard it is to get a woman off. It can take some of them ten, twenty minutes. Who has time for that? Am I right? Well, I suppose men like you do. So after she's with child, have at her."

The red drained from Graham's vision. It was replaced with a clear view of the situation. Raveena would walk circles around this man. She wouldn't even have to run. The Snow Queen would eat this golden prince alive with silk-gloved fingers and a smile that could freeze rivers.

Charming didn't see it—couldn't see it. Too stupid. Too arrogant. He thought bedding the queen meant ruling beside her.

Fool.

Graham knew better. He knew how to make Raveena kneel before him. How to make her beg him. How to get her to concede. Because she knew, without a single doubt in that beautiful mind of hers, that his every move on the game board was to get her the win. The orgasm. The prize.

This boy might be a prince. But Graham was the king. A king without a crown. For his queen to have the ultimate prize, she would have to marry this idiot.

Graham was going to have to let her.

"You almost had me near the end of our bout." Charming tugged on his shirt—crimson velvet embroidered with gold that caught the firelight like a smug smirk. "That move near the end?" He mimicked a feint with his hand. "Could've taken my head off."

Graham still hadn't moved, still hadn't spoken a single word. Not that Charming had noticed. Graham stood with his boots planted squarely on the queen's side of the threshold, arms crossed, spine rigid.

"But then," Charming continued, buttoning his cuffs, "you dropped to your knees."

He turned then, fully dressed and insufferably pleased with himself. His polished boots stopped just shy of crossing into Raveena's rooms. He stood toe to toe with Graham, not that it made them equals.

"There's been talk that you might've thrown the match, let me win. You and I both know no true warrior would ever show his neck to a lesser opponent."

Graham's jaw flexed. His fingers twitched once— just once—where they rested on his biceps. A wolf would have snapped his teeth. Graham didn't even blink.

Charming chuckled, mistaking the silence for surrender. He turned, smug and satisfied, unaware how close he'd walked to the edge of something deadly. But the prince didn't get too far.

A guard stood in the outer door to the king's chambers. The man was dressed in the gold of Charming's lands, but he was followed by men in the ice blue of Thornhall.

"Your highness, you must come," said one of the golden guards.

The golden guards led Charming away. The Thornhall guards stayed behind to face Graham.

"What?" Graham barked.

It had to do with Snow White. Had they found the princess? Had they been wrong? Had it been foul play?

"The queen. She's gone."

CHAPTER TWENTY-ONE

Raveena stirred as the creaking groan of iron wheels slowed beneath her. Her head pounded a sharp, throbbing ache behind her temples. Her mouth was dry with the bitter aftertaste of magic.

The carriage door opened, spilling pale moonlight inside. Flame-red hair filled her vision. Her captor's serene face came into view. The girl didn't look entirely human. Her chin was too sharp, her ears a bit pointy. There were slits at her neck like gills. Most telling, she smelled like the bitter magic of a witch and the salty depths of the sea.

"Siren," Raveena guessed.

The girl kept her mouth shut. It was good that she didn't speak again. Not when the first song still rang in

Raveena's ears. At least she was awake now and under her own faculties. But how long would that last?

Princess Aurora stood beside the redhead, who Raveena had to guess was the Sea Princess Ariel. So she knew the players. Now she just had to figure out the game.

"Where am I?" Raveena asked.

"The Forbidden Forest," Aurora answered softly, as though not to disturb the monsters sleeping within.

Raveena turned in a slow circle. Her skirts rustled against the frost-laced underbrush. The air here was damp, dense. The trees loomed like watchful sentinels. Icicles hung from twisted limbs that clawed at the moonlight as if trying to snatch the stars from the sky. Somewhere in the distance, an animal called out. It was a sharp, keening cry that scraped down her spine like a blade. Another call answered, lower and closer, and then was abruptly cut off.

Eyes blinked in the darkness. Dozens. Maybe more. Gold, silver, green—reflections of wild things, waiting things, hungry things.

Her boots sank in the mossy soil with each step, the earth too soft, as if it might open beneath her feet. The scent of decay clung to the wind, sweet and rotting, like overripe fruit left too long in a gilded bowl.

She had never set foot in the Forbidden Forest before. It wasn't a place for queens and politics. This was ancient ground, older than any throne. She was a queen on the wrong board, surrounded by pieces she hadn't placed in a game she hadn't agreed to play. But she refused to be anyone's pawn.

"This is Snow's plan? Have you two displaced princesses play nursemaids while she storms the castle gates?"

The two girls exchanged a glance. Not one of triumph. One of unease. Ariel looked like she was regretting everything. Aurora's mouth was pressed into a thin, uncertain line.

"We didn't bring you here to hold you," Aurora said. "Snow's not out storming the castle. We brought you here to take her back with you. To take all of us back with you."

Raveena blinked. Her mouth parted. No words came.

They turned, leading her toward a small, lopsided house tucked into a clearing. The forest wrapped around it like a protective spell, hush and shadow between the trees. Ivy curled along the wood-planked windows. Smoke drifted from the chimney in a lazy ribbon.

The door creaked their arrival when Ariel opened it, the worn hinges groaning like an old sentinel roused from sleep. Inside, the cottage was dim but warm, the hearth alive with amber light. Seven chairs, each slightly different in height and carving, ringed the long wooden table. Behind them, seven axes hung on pegs by the door, blades clean but well-used, their handles worn smooth by familiar hands.

Woven rugs softened the stone floors. Jars of herbs lined the shelves beside tin cups and sturdy plates. A set of embroidered curtains—clumsily stitched but clearly an effort at beauty—framed the back window. There was a kettle steaming over the fire. Tucked into the corners were signs of domestic care: a basket of mended socks, a pile of polished stones arranged like decoration, and the lingering scent of lavender and cedar.

A woman had been here. Or at least, a woman's touch.

"The domesticity of it all makes my stomach hurt," Aurora said under her breath.

Raveena's gaze lingered on a chipped ceramic bowl full of ripe berries, then moved to the set of hooks by the door, each holding a different colored cloak. Order, despite the wildness outside. Safety, despite the blades.

Snow White paced across the wooden floor, her raven black hair tangled, her gown wrinkled. She turned as the door opened and froze. Her eyes met Raveena's—and flared with betrayal.

"You… you brought her here? I can't believe the two of you betrayed me after all I've done for you."

"Exactly what have you done for us, Snow?" Aurora spread her hands around the small cabin. "We came seeking refuge in a castle, and you bring us to a cramped cottage."

"It's not cramped. There's plenty of room and all the wide open space of the forest."

Ariel and Aurora shared another look. Ariel's fingers began to move in rapid fire. Aurora watched those hands and spoke as though she were translating. "We're royalty, not ruffians. Our idea of roughing it is a manor house, not a hovel."

Ariel's hands stopped, but Aurora wasn't done. She turned to Snow with words of her own. "And to top that off, you're in an active war with a queen. We told you we're done fighting. We just want our happy ending to begin."

"Excuse me, ladies." Raveena cleared her throat and held up one finger as though making a point of order. "You'll forgive me, but I'm having trouble keeping up. I thought you were running a coup."

Snow turned her back, raking trembling fingers through her hair. "This would have all been over if that stupid huntsman had just killed you."

Raveena blinked. "I beg your pardon, darling?"

Huntsman? She couldn't mean Graham. Graham would never put a blade to her…

"You didn't really think I was going to let the fact

that you murdered my father slide. Did you, Step-mother, dear?"

This again. Raveena sighed. She supposed she should come clean about what really happened the night that the king drew his last breath. But Snow wasn't done. In fact, she was just getting started.

"My father was a good man." Snow raised her hands as she spoke, and magic unfurled from her fingertips.

At the window, the trees groaned, their limbs clawing against the panes like impatient fists. A dark shape moved through the underbrush—a hulking figure on all fours, its breath fogging the glass. Above, the chimney shrieked with the sound of birds wheeling and crying. From within the cracks and hollows of the rundown cottage walls came the frantic skittering of claws.

Mice. Dozens of them. They poured out from the floorboards, from between loose stones and beneath the hearth, charging toward her like a wave of fur and teeth.

Raveena lifted her hands and dropped the temper-ature with a single breath. The air crackled. Ice spiraled from her fingertips, painting the ground in a curling frost. It crystallized along the beams and windows. With a vicious gust, she swept her arms upward.

The mice screamed. Tiny, high-pitched cries as they

were lifted in a spinning vortex of snow and sent hurtling up the chimney in a flurry of soot and ash.

The room fell briefly silent. Until the front door creaked open. Hulking and bristling with steam was the form of a bear. One massive paw landed on the first step.

Raveena exhaled. The air hissed with cold. Frost bloomed beneath the bear's paw, and with a growl, it lost traction—slipping violently, its weight crashing down into the frozen earth with a furious roar.

She turned back to Snow and raised a brow. This was the kind of game she was used to. There was a bit of pride in her chest that her stepdaughter was at least matching her and not making the game boring.

"Your father died in his sleep. He was old. His heart stopped from his… exertions."

"You lie." Snow raised both arms, and the trees trembled. Glass shattered. A murder of crows came screaming into the room and aimed at Raveena. They circled her like shadows with teeth.

Wind howled through the cottage, clawing at curtains and sending ash swirling up from the hearth. With the windows open, Raveena pulled the icicles from tree branches into the room. Wind whipped around her. Crystals formed in the air.

The birds shrieked, wings beating frantically against the gale as they tried to scatter. But they were too slow.

The first impaled a crow mid-cry, pinning it to the timber beam above with a sickening crunch. Another punched through a raven's chest, feathers exploding in a wet burst of black and red. Blood streaked the walls. The scent of copper and snow filled the air. One by one, the birds were speared at the end of the frozen blades.

Snow gaped. "Murderer."

"Well, the birds, yes. But not your father. I was beneath him when it happened. I swore the servants to secrecy. Because can you imagine the embarrassment?"

Snow wasn't listening. She flung out her hand toward the open door, commanding the wilderness like a conductor summoning a crescendo. The bear, still frozen at the foot of the steps, bellowed and thrashed, claws carving furrows into the ice-slick ground. Another sound split the air—a long, mournful howl that echoed through the trees like a warning bell.

Between the snow-laden trunks, shapes emerged. Low to the ground, sinewed and silent, the wolves came. Half-seen shadows at first, then flesh and fur— thick coats dusted in frost, muscles rippling beneath. Their eyes glowed with a feral yellow light, twin moons ringed in black. Lips curled back to reveal teeth, white and gleaming like bone, saliva threading between them as pink tongues licked hungrily at the cold air.

They moved in tandem, circling, paws pressing silently into the snow. One stepped forward, shoulders hunched, nose twitching as it caught the scent of blood, of magic, of war.

And then—

They saw her.

The wolves took one look at Raveena and paused. The one in front, the alpha of the pack, sniffed the air. His gaze narrowed on her. Then he bowed his head and turned. The others followed suit, walking back into the dark forest.

Another howl rent the air, this time from the dark-haired princess. Snow charged. She moved like a tempest of fury and grief, a blade of rage and memory. It was woman against woman now.

Raveena met her head-on. Their hands clashed. Magic surged as their bodies went out the door, over the head of the bear, and fell at the roots of an ancient tree.

Snow's fingernails tore through Raveena's shoulder. Raveena's frost burned red welts along Snow's arms. They twisted, grappled, eyes locked.

Snow's boot caught Raveena's knee. Raveena snarled and threw her off with a blast of snow that knocked them both apart. Snow stumbled, regained her footing, and raised her hand—

Then froze.

Her face twisted.

She dropped to her knees with a cry—not of pain

from battle but something deeper, stranger.

Raveena blinked through the haze of magic. "Snow?"

Snow crawled to the base of a tree and retched.

The forest went utterly still. Even the birds stopped crying.

Raveena rose slowly, her power ebbing. The ice receded, melting into dew.

Aurora and Ariel ducked their heads from their hiding spaces. It was Aurora that spoke up. "She's been irrational like this since she found out she's pregnant."

CHAPTER TWENTY-TWO

Cold bit at the edges of Graham's cloak. He didn't feel it. Not when the scent of her still lingered in the air.

He crouched low at the spot where the carriage had departed, his callused fingers brushing over the faint indentations in the snow. The horses had left clean tracks. No scuffle. No signs of a chase. No blood. Only the sharp, orderly trail of wheels and hooves rolling away from the castle gates like a secret leaving in the night.

Graham leaned closer, nostrils flaring. The scent was wrong. It wasn't frostbitten lilies or curling smoke. It wasn't the crisp, glacial signature of her magic. No, this was something else.

He inhaled again and tasted…salt. Not the kind

mined from caves or laced in a nobleman's meal. Sea salt. Brine. Magic that crashed like waves and pulled like tides.

The ocean had touched this. Had she been taken by someone from the Coastal Kingdom? Or perhaps the Sea Kingdom? But again, no signs of struggle.

She must be playing a game. But if she was, she would have left him a sign, a hint. That is, if she truly saw him as a partner.

A howl broke across the stillness. Low, mournful, stretched thin with distance. The hair along the back of Graham's neck prickled. His ears, attuned beyond human measure, turned toward the sound. The wolf's call came from the south.

He stood, breath clouding around him. The Forbidden Forest lay that way.

"It appears there's been foul play." Prince Charming strode forward with his usual smugness masked as concern. He wore the king's crown like a boy playing dress-up, the tips of it too high for his brow. "Both Queen Raveena and Princess Snow are missing. I suspect the work of traitors—or worse. I will send the queen's guards east. We will smoke them out and bring our girls back safely."

The noblewomen had gathered, cloaked in opulence. Their fur muffs and velvet hoods framed pale faces and curious eyes. Jewels winked at their throats and wrists, glinting like icicles in the moonlight. Their perfumes clashed on the breeze—spiced amber, rosewater, and powdered musk. None of them masked the absence Graham felt in his bones.

"Gather your men and leave at once, Huntsman."

Graham didn't move. Didn't blink. He kept his gaze trained on the dark stretch in the distance that was the start of the Forbidden Forest.

Why would she go in there? Like most queens, Raveena hated the outdoors. Unless she knew that's where Snow had gone off to.

"Did you not hear your king, soldier? Rally your men and head east at once."

"They went south."

Charming gave a sharp, incredulous laugh. "Preposterous. My trackers already made their assessment. They used the best magical mapping tech in all the realms—charms from Valebright, spellstone from the Inland mages. East is the logical route. That's where they'll be."

"I used my eyes. My ears. My nose," Graham growled. "And they all point south."

Charming stepped forward, finger wagging like a petulant schoolmaster. "Mind your king, soldier, or—"

Graham cut him off by grabbing the front of his finely embroidered doublet and lifting him clean off the ground. The prince's boots dangled for a heartbeat before Graham set him aside like a child throwing a tantrum, placing him firmly out of his way.

Then Graham turned his back on the prince. Because Charming didn't matter. He stepped toward the crescent of queens and noblewomen.

"There was no struggle. No overturned wheels. No blood in the snow. Only two sets of tracks leading south." His gaze swept across the women. "They went willingly."

A hush rippled through the court. The crackle of the torches sounded suddenly loud, the frost-bitten air razor-thin.

"I don't know what game Snow and Raveena are playing." A few brows rose at the use of the royal women's given names. Graham was too close to the edge to stand on ceremony. "But the Forbidden Forest is no place to make their moves."

He took another step forward, into the ring of power, his eyes hard. "I'm going south to get my queen back. And I'll checkmate anyone—queen, prince, or pawn—who tries to stop me."

Silence. Even the wind held its breath.

Lady Charming lifted her foot as though to take a step forward. She was fuming, red-faced and trembling with words unsaid. But she didn't speak. Because the other ladies tilted their heads. No words. Just the slow, deliberate incline of chins.

One by one, crowns dipped, acknowledging Graham's request. Even though it wasn't a request. It was simply notice.

Graham turned on his heel, snow crunching beneath his boots, and strode into the dark.

Toward the forest.

Toward her.

CHAPTER TWENTY-THREE

The long wooden table was scarred with age, its surface marred by blade nicks and scorches from the battle that had torn through the cottage only moments ago. The fire in the hearth hadn't forgotten. It snapped and hissed, spitting resin and throwing flickers of warmth into a room that still smelled of burned feathers.

Raveena sat stiff-backed at the table, her hands wrapped loosely around a carved wooden cup of untouched tea. Birds fluttered about the rafters, cawing in frantic whispers as they tucked sprigs of moss and hay back into the places Raveena's ice had shattered. Squirrels scrambled over the mantle, sweeping away soot with their tails. Even the mice had returned, though they shot her wary glances before scurrying across the floor to drag away the tiny corpses of their avian comrades. One bird, its wing speared through by an icicle, was carted off with solemn care.

The bear sat at the front window like a sentry, massive and brooding, its thick bulk blocking out the worst of the frigid air that howled down from the mountains. Its breath fogged the glass.

Aurora had brewed the tea—chamomile and some forest herb that made the steam smell like crushed apples. She'd handed it to Snow, who sat curled in a chair by the fire. Her pale hands had a death grip around the mug. She hadn't looked at Raveena once since the announcement of her condition.

Aurora took a seat beside Ariel. Their fingers entwined atop the table. Their closeness was a language of its own.

"We were supposed to be poisoned," said Aurora. "Put to sleep. Have our voices taken. Then promised off to men who didn't know our names and kissed us without consent. That's what this world had in store for us. Can you blame us for fighting back?"

Ariel pulled her hand from Aurora's and began making signs. Aurora translated.

"We just want to be left alone. To live in peace. To love one another. Not the person that was written in the storybooks for us to wed and be miserable ever after. That's all."

Ariel folded her hands in her lap.

"And a manor, if it's not too much trouble," Aurora added. "Or a cottage with indoor plumbing, maybe?"

Raveena said nothing. She didn't look at them. Her eyes were on Snow.

A cut marred the princess's brow—just above the bone, where her dark hair was matted with blood. It wasn't deep, but it stood out in the firelight, raw and red and defiant. Raveena rose from her seat and crossed the room.

She sat beside Snow slowly, waiting for the girl to flinch, to pull away.

Snow didn't. She only tensed.

Raveena lifted a hand. When her fingers brushed the girl's cheek, Snow jerked… then stilled. Magic pulsed through her fingertips, cool and gentle. The cut closed beneath her touch.

"You really didn't kill him?" Snow's voice was fragile. Not like glass—glass was too clean. It was more like cracked ice on a lake: fractured and dangerous beneath the surface.

"It was his time. He died in bed. No poison. No daggers."

"You never loved him." It wasn't a question.

Raveena's gaze dropped to the fire. "My heart was… somewhere else."

Snow gave a hollow, brittle laugh. "I always assumed

you'd cut it out of your own chest. I didn't believe you'd willingly given it away."

It was the truth. Raveena's heart had never belonged to the man who gave her a throne. It belonged to the wolf who gave her freedom.

"I'll make a deal with you," Raveena said. "We'll be allies. You and Prince Charming will move to Valebright. I'll keep Thornhall and—"

"No!"

Raveena sighed. War was the last thing she wanted with her stepdaughter. She'd give up the crown but not the castle.

"You heard what they just said." Snow gestured to Aurora and Ariel. "Did it not move you even a little?"

The princesses' words had moved Raveena. More than she cared to admit. If it ever did come to a choice between keeping the castle or keeping Graham… well… she wasn't going to say her choice out loud. But it was crystal clear to her whose warmth she wanted to be wrapped up inside on the cold winter nights.

"Why do I still have to marry Charming?"

Raveena's gaze dipped to Snow's stomach. "Because you're carrying his child."

Silence fell like a guillotine. From the corner of her eye, Raveena saw Ariel and Aurora exchange a glance. Quick. Tight. Nervous.

She turned back to Snow. "It is Charming's child?"

Snow hesitated. Her fingers curled around the mug. She shook her head.

"Whose, then?"

A glance around the little cottage gave Raveena her answer. The walls of axed wood, carved furniture, animal skins. Seven chairs, all perfectly sized for the small men who lived here.

"The father is a dwarf?"

Snow's throat bobbed as she swallowed. She gave a tiny nod.

Raveena took in a long, deep breath that expanded her lungs and lifted her chest. Inside the castle's keep, no one dared comment on a queen's bed partners. Not when they were young noblemen. Not when they were rugged commoners.

But a dwarf? That choice was going to be a bridge other queens might not be willing to cross.

"There are seven of them, darling. Which one is the father?"

Snow winced. She bit her lower lip. When she lifted her gaze to meet Raveena's, the Snow Queen realized a truth she had never fathomed. Pure little Snow White was even further from the innocent everyone had believed the girl to be.

CHAPTER TWENTY-FOUR

The trees of the Forbidden Forest twisted like skeletal hands, gnarled and blackened by frost, their limbs creaking beneath the weight of snow and shadow. Graham moved through them with the stealth of a predator, boots crunching over ice-laced leaves, breath pluming from his mouth like smoke from a dragon's maw.

Every sense was on edge. His ears tuned to the rustle of branches. His nose flaring for scent. His blade already drawn and slick with condensation from the cold.

Something was behind him. Not human. The forest had long ago swallowed the footsteps of men, replacing them with things untamed. He could feel it—eyes watching, tracking.

He stopped in a small clearing where the moonlight barely touched the snow, just enough to paint the frost in silver and blue. He turned slowly, every muscle taut, and raised his sword.

Nothing.

Only silence. The thick, shrouded kind of silence that made the world feel as though it had forgotten to breathe.

Then a crack snapped through the trees. Graham spun, blade at the ready. But it wasn't an attack. It was her.

Raveena's scent threaded through the cold like a ribbon of fire. He'd been following it for an hour, his compass through the chaos. But now it had veered. She had changed course.

He growled low in his throat and pivoted in the direction of her new trail—just in time to see movement at the edge of the trees. A blur of pale fur and golden eyes.

A wolf.

It stood still, half-shadowed. The muscles in its shoulders were tight beneath a rime-crusted coat. The animal's gaze met his—intelligent, unwavering. It wasn't an alpha male. It was an alpha female.

It wasn't issuing a threat or a challenge. This was a summons.

"Commander!" a voice called from behind.

Graham turned. Corwin emerged from the brush, followed by three of his men, all wearing the grime and worry of a hard march. Snow crusted their boots and stuck in their beards.

"We found her," Corwin said, panting. "We think the princess is in the dwarves' cabin."

"The dwarves?" Graham's gaze went south to the dwarves' cabin, then to the west where he'd picked up Raveena's new trail.

What would they be doing there? The dwarves would be in the mines this time of year. Weeks before they'd surface again. This game board made less and less sense with each move.

Graham's gaze flicked back to the wolf. Still watching. Still waiting. "You four—go to the cottage. Secure the princess."

Corwin hesitated. "And you?"

"I don't think the queen is there. I'm following her." Graham nodded to the wolf. "She's taking me to my queen."

Corwin looked as if he might protest, but one glance at Graham's face and he appeared to think better of it. With a curt salute, he and the others disappeared into the trees.

Graham turned back to the wolf. She'd already begun to move, padding silently through the forest, barely leaving a print behind.

They moved fast, weaving through gorges, ducking beneath ice-laden branches, skimming the edge of frozen ravines. The forest whispered to itself, its secrets carried on the wind, its breath thick with old magic. The deeper they went, the wilder the world became. No paths. No markers. Just instinct and hunger and the moon.

They broke from the trees at last, the canopy splitting wide to reveal a cliff edge crowned in snow. The wind caught him hard in the chest, cold enough to steal breath.

And there she was.

Raveena stood on the precipice, her back to him, hair whipping like a pale banner in the wind. She was surrounded by wolves, their bodies sleek and still, forming a protective ring around her like living sentinels. The moon bathed her in argent light, casting her in silver and shadow, queen of frost and fury.

"You found me."

"I will always find you, my queen."

The wolves turned as one, ears flicking, bodies tensing. He felt their eyes on him, felt their judgment pass over him like a gust of wind.

Graham stepped forward, slow and measured. One wolf, larger than the others, bared its teeth in warning. Graham met its gaze without flinching. He let them see the fire in him. The devotion that no frost could quell.

The tension stretched taut between man and beast—until, one by one, they stepped aside.

He prowled forward until he was within reach of her—until her scent filled his lungs and the cold radiating from her skin made the air between them sting.

"That's your game board down there," she said. "Your seat of power."

Below them, nestled in the valley, was Greymoor. That land was empty of civilization, a canvas ready to be painted upon by men like him. A place without queens and kings. Which lead Graham to question if it would ever be a place for him.

"Want to play a game, huntsman?"

CHAPTER TWENTY-FIVE

The huntsman's cottage creaked with the weight of time. Its walls, bowed from years of wind and snow, groaned as the door opened with a protesting wail. Dust hung thick in the air, glittering like frost in the weak moonlight that spilled through warped glass panes. There was no warmth waiting for them here—no fire, no fur, nothing but shadows.

Raveena had never needed warmth. She was the winter.

She stepped inside first, her boots cracking over frost-bitten floorboards. Her breath left her in a visible puff. She raised her hands, fingers glinting with ice-laced magic. With a flick of her wrist, the chill in the air recoiled. The cold clung stubbornly for a moment, like a child not yet ready to be dismissed, before it was drawn out through the cracks and seams of the house. Windows fogged, then cleared. Frost retreated from the walls. The air settled, cool but no longer biting.

She turned slowly, her pale gaze catching on the man who filled the doorway like a dark storm. Graham. Her wolf. Her person. Her peace.

She reached for the hem of her gown and pulled the garment up and over her head. The rest followed—layer by layer, each piece shed until she stood bare in the center of the room. Then she knelt.

The Snow Queen bent the knee for the only man who had ever commanded her body. The only man who knew how. Her palms rested on her thighs, her spine straight, chin tilted up so her eyes could meet his.

This was their game. Her offering. His power. And gods, how she loved when he took control.

She waited. Breath held. A smile curving like mischief on her lips.

Graham didn't make the move she expected. That thrilled her all the more. He approached—yes—but not like a conqueror. Not like the wild thing that had pinned her to stone walls and held her down while delivering bruising kisses. He walked past her.

Having him out of sight only increased her desire. Liquid heat pooled between her thighs. She wanted to look down and check if a puddle was forming on the hard floor.

Graham crouched behind her. She heard a rustle of fabric. That's when she turned.

He picked up her gown first. He shook it out with a snap, letting the skirt billow like a wave before folding it along its seams with surprising precision. Fingers rough from battle moved with the delicacy of a court seamstress. He placed the gown on the seat of a rickety wooden chair, smoothing the bodice with his palm until the wrinkles gave way.

He draped her stockings over the high back of the chair so they'd dry in the warmth she had summoned into the room. Lastly, her shoes. He set them side by side beneath the chair, perfectly aligned, as if they were soldiers standing at attention. Then he turned his attention to her.

His prowl toward her was a slow march. His gaze held her captive. When he reached her, Raveena tilted her chin higher, waiting for his command. For the leash of his hands around her neck. For the rough toss of her body on the bed before he fucked her into submission.

"I love you, Ray."

Raveena flinched. He had never once said those words out loud to her. She supposed she knew it on some level. To hear it tossed at her so casually was a shock to the system.

"I love you when you are fire and fury. I love you when you freeze the world to its bones. I love you when you rule from a throne. I love you now, kneeling on bare floorboards in a forgotten cabin."

Her chest rose with a trembling inhale. This wasn't their game. There were no veiled commands, no submission laced with hunger, no careful, calculated power exchanged in silence.

This was raw. Unmasked. And it terrified her.

"I will be your sword or your shield. Your bed or your battleground. Whatever you need for the rest of our lives."

Graham reached down. He didn't put his hand around her throat. He didn't thrust his fingers into her weeping core. His palms found her waist. Rough hands gentled as he brought her to her feet.

She looked up at him, no longer grinning. She met his gaze not with tears or with tenderness but with the steel of a woman who had always survived by staying untouched by softness.

"What game are you playing, huntsman?"

"The game is over, my queen. I let you win for the last time."

"Let me—"

He scooped her up into his arms. Raveena let out a sigh of relief. Now they were getting somewhere. But he didn't toss her onto the bed. He set her down... gently.

"Stop this," she demanded. "We don't do foreplay."

"I told you, I'm not playing with you."

Raveena balled her hand into a fist and aimed it for his chest. Graham caught it easily. He stretched first one arm over her head and then gathered up the other and followed suit.

Raveena breathed a sigh of relief that was heavy with desire. This was what she wanted. His control. His command.

Graham gave her his kisses. But these weren't the kisses she had come to crave. These were soft caresses at the corner of her eyelids. They were whisper light at the tip of her nose. It cracked something inside her, a fissure blooming wide and sudden beneath her ribs. Her heart surged against it, trying to crawl up into her throat, trying to become something she could speak or scream or swallow.

"Graham, don't," she warned.

He ignored her. He let one wrist go. She bared her teeth, ready to lash out with her free hand, demanding that he recapture it and hold her firm. Then she realized it was only to gather her wrist with his other hand. With his free hand, he reached between them to free his hard length.

Once again, Raveena felt a surge of relief tinged with desire. His big head might be playing with her, but his even bigger head would take her side in this battle. Graham's cock was built for conquering, not caresses.

However, when the head of his weapon nudged her entrance, it did so carefully, asking for permission. Not barging in.

"No," she hissed.

Graham progressed inch by inch. Raveena struggled against him, raising her hips to take all of him at once. But he was too big, too strong. She was helpless against his tenderness.

She was getting what she wanted but not how she wanted it. He was inside her. Filling her over and again. His thrusts were a steady, relentless siege on every wall she'd ever raised. One by one, they came crumbling down.

He'd said this wasn't a game. He'd said he wasn't going to let her win any longer. And now she understood the consequences of the game that they were not playing.

This wasn't a game of bed sport. Graham was a man of action. He'd said the words, and now he was making good on his word and making love to her.

"Stop," she pleaded.

"No," he said with a kiss to her temple and a deep thrust inside her.

"I can't."

"You already do."

It was three against one. Their two bodies moved in perfect cadence, not in submission but in communion

—two warriors carving a sacred truce into flesh and breath and rhythm. Graham's mouth was the leader of this coup. It was only Raveena's mind—her sense of self-preservation that had kept a crown on her head for all these years—that was a raging opponent.

"Don't worry, Ray. I won't make you say it."

Saying it was nothing. It was feeling it that was tearing her apart. Deep beneath the armor Raveena had worn for so long it had become a second skin, something fragile unfurled. A pressure built behind her eyes. She tried to blink it away. It wouldn't be banished.

It gathered instead—light as frost, heavy as grief. A tear. Just one. A single snowflake of sorrow and surrender and joy, all folded into a perfect crystal. She let it slip free. It was the first she'd ever shed. It very well might be the last.

At the sight of it, Graham stopped. He had seen her blood before. Had kissed bruises and salt and snow from her skin. But never this.

He leaned in, reverent. His tongue brushed the path the tear traced along her cheek. He caught it before it reached her chin and closed his mouth around it like a sacrament. His eyes burned into hers, wolf-bright and wide with awe, as though he had just tasted proof of a miracle.

Raveena put her hand on his chest. Beneath her palm, his skin was warm and taut, his breath shallow, waiting. And there it was, steady and strong, the *thump-thump* of a heart.

Snow had called her heartless. She hadn't denied it. She had placed her heart away in the one place it could beat happily, ever after.

Their lips met. The kiss didn't burn or bruise. It bloomed, opening like frost melting under the spring sun. No battle this time. No victory to claim. Just two sovereigns surrendering to the peace they'd carved with blood and will and the refusal to yield to anything less than everything.

Graham's body moved over hers in rhythm, not as a conqueror but as a partner. Each thrust a conversation, each sigh an answer. Her hips rose to meet him, not in defiance but in accord. They matched one another move for move, breath for breath, the old dance made new by meaning.

Her fingers clung tightly to his. He held on just as fiercely. When release came, it was not a cry of triumph but a shared exhale of completion. A final, perfect surrender. Fingers still laced, hearts still in synch, they reached the end together—equal, whole… home.

Yes. Home.

As Graham pulled Raveena onto his back in that strange way he had of cuddling with her, she decided to ask the question that had sprung into her mind since the wolves had led her away from the Forbidden Forest to this untouched stretch of land.

"Would you do anything for me?"

"Does it involve killing your stepdaughter?"

"Snow has enough problems on her plate. But I think she'll get through it. She'll need my help, of course. Though I don't do diapers."

"Diapers?"

"Answer my question."

"Yes, I would do anything for you, my love."

"Would you build me a castle?"

ABOUT INES JOHNSON

Lover of fairytales, folklore, and mythology, Ines Johnson spends her days reimagining the stories of old in a modern world. She writes books where damsels cause the distress, princesses wield swords, and moms save the world.

If you liked Ines' Beast then you'll love her Vampires and Dragons. To find out more just visit https://ineswrites.com/ReaderGroup

Want More FANTASY ROMANCE by INES JOHNSON?

Wicked Evermore
Wicked Beauty
Wicked Song
Wicked Chill

The Lunaterra Chronicles

The Beastly Crown
The Beautiful Blade

Immortal Vices and Virtues
Forbid Me
Reveal Me